Thirty years ago, Baldo Scarpa had built a name for himself—a name that had inspired awe among small-time mobsters who were used to taking orders, and feared men like Scarpa who were used to giving them out.

But the name the underworld honored was anathema to the law, and when it caught up with Scarpa, he paid the price for crime—ten thousand nights in prison.

One man waited for Scarpa's parole, a man who needed the one-time great name of Baldo Scarpa to front for him in a narcotics deal which could make him rich. And Scarpa needed a friend, one who remembered the old days, even if the old days were long gone and the friend was a cheap crook whose greed could send Scarpa back to prison, a four-time loser. . . .

FOUR-TIME LOSER

by Dan Lynch

WILDSIDE PRESS

FOUR-TIME LOSER

Suppose a man is my age?"

Baldo Scarpa put the question without feeling, containing within himself a fascination, a dread for what lay in the answer. It was late afternoon in spring in the great prison at Dannemora, and the sun cast a shadow of steel bars on the white painted walls of the infirmary. Dr. Martin Croy considered the question.

"How old is that?" he asked.

"Old enough," Baldo Scarpa answered. "Maybe old enough to be your father."

Dr. Croy smiled. "Let me see?"

Baldo was seated on a bench with a group of silent men, all waiting to be selected for the one hopeful way out of the walls; all lifers, sentenced by judges in different parts of the state for long stretches that would eat out their lives. Luther Williams, a sandhog, had come to the big jail from somewhere on the Great Lakes, sentenced for the axe murder of his wife. Williams was a leathery, muscular man with an enormous bald crown surrounded by freckles and a fringe of reddish hair. He had been panting noisily and some of his tension had infected the rest of the prisoners. Over the years, he and Baldo had become friends—so far as anyone in the big prison could make friendships—and their appearance today at the infirmary had been the result of long and mutually enlightened exchanges.

"One thing can happen," Luther had argued. "If the worst comes, it's the shoe laces and a quick out. The other way, a pardon and you walk through the gate."

Baldo shook his head. "Cancer," he said forebodingly. "Eh? Not so good!"

7

Still, there was the chance given to the prisoners by a compassionate state. Medical science needed human guinea pigs. Monkeys, white rats, hamsters, mice, all had gone as far as they could in the interests of humanity, and now human flesh and tissue were needed. Volunteers were wanted.

"You go," Williams said, "I go!"

"I got to think," Baldo said.

"I don't get it," Williams said wonderingly.

Baldo said, "Don't get what?"

That conversation, Baldo recalled, had taken place in the great yard where the convicts were permitted to put up huts of corrugated tin, wood planking, and other odds and ends borrowed or stolen from the workshops. Perhaps an acre was devoted to the recreational facility, and the order, or disorder, had the appearance of a mining camp. Small fires were going and coffee was being brewed in tin cans and makeshift containers. A haze of smoke rose over the walls and drifted across the wooded hills of the Adirondack mountains. The fact that Baldo's own hut, knocked together from packing cases, had several feet of privacy indicated something of his status. Luther Williams called attention to this.

"You!" Williams said. "A nothing like me, yeah! I got to take any way out. Cancer or no cancer. But Scarpa? I know all about you."

"What do you know?" Baldo asked.

Williams grunted. "Big. You're big."

Baldo frowned. "Who said that?"

"Malfino."

Williams was referring to Carl Malfino, a young convict who had recently been released from the prison. Baldo turned a sharp glance to his fellow convict.

"Malfino?" he frowned. "What did he have to say?"

Williams was taken aback by the sharp tone. He finished a can of coffee and stared at coarse grounds. "Not too much. Malfino claims he knows you from the neighborhood. You got a lovely daughter. Name of Helen."

Baldo's stare had a deadly quality. "Yeah, I got a daughter," he replied.

"You never talk about that."

"No."

Williams shrugged. "Your business."

A moment of silence passed, interrupted only by the hacking cough of a convict in a nearby hut. Baldo said, "Why would he talk about that?"

"Just said she's got a kid and you got a home to go to," Williams replied. "You were big," he added. "So why can't you walk out?"

Baldo's eyes closed. "I was the biggest," he said grimly. "Long time ago and nobody remembers."

"Malfino remembers," Williams said, and shivered. "He gives me the creeps."

"Why?"

"Always pumping."

Baldo was silent. "I been up and down to the governor for that pardon with the biggest lawyers. It cost a fortune and it don't help. I was too big. Without a good reason, they won't do business with Baldo. They remember that stink the time they let Lucky walk out. Governors come, governors go. I'm in this hole for life." His hand touched a photograph of a child, a solemn girl with black eyes, resting in his pocket. "But cancer? I ain't sure I want that way out."

"It would give the governor a reason," Williams said.

Baldo set an iron mouth. "I got to think!" The phrase persisted down to the day when he found himself in the infirmary with a handful of nervous convicts waiting for the doctor to speak. Aloud he said, "I got to think."

But even as he protested, he knew he would go along with the request. Baldo Scarpa had come to a point where he would rather die than do time. He faced the man in the white coat thoughtfully.

"What I got to do?" he demanded.

Dr. Croy shrugged and directed his answer to the group as a whole. "It's as simple as this, Baldo," he said, keeping his gaze on the fierce old man before him. "Next month we're starting a research project in skin cancer—a special strain of cancer cells we've been growing in glass at the laboratory. It's a new technique. Follow me?"

"Eh? Sure!"

Baldo nodded with silent contempt. The doctor, an outsider, was patronizing his intelligence, on the theory that a man with a record was deficient in feeling or intelligence, or both. But the fact was that Baldo Scarpa was far ahead of the doctor. He was an intelligent man with a shrewd understanding of the world he lived in. A world, he thought with grim satisfaction, which would have swallowed up the smooth-faced doctor without a trace.

Baldo added, "You're keeping the cancer alive. Just like you keep the germs. In the little glass jars."

"Why, yes!"

Dr. Croy nodded and went on to explain the purpose of the experiment. While the cause of cancer was unknown, certain cases of spontaneous remission from the disease had led the medical team working out of Cornell Medical School to hypothesize a body substance specifically deadly to cancer cells. Two things would happen at once; a certain biochemical substance would be injected in the blood stream of the volunteer, and simultaneously an implant would be made under the skin of cancerous tissue taken from a terminal case in the great research center in New York City.

"Then what?" Luther Williams called out.

Dr. Croy turned to explain the close supervision of the medical team. Either the body would reject the implant, or the cancer would take root and flourish. In that case, it would be promptly excised and treated with X-rays and the latest drugs.

"If it don't work?" Williams asked.

Dr. Croy shrugged. "You're lifers, aren't you?" he asked briefly. "And volunteers. In all likelihood, the body defenses will reject the implant. There's a chance it won't."

"We ain't animals," Williams said.

Dr. Croy replied, "We don't ask animals. We're asking you."

Baldo Scarpa stared grimly at the steel bars of the infirmary. "Where do I sign?" he demanded. "I can think of something worse than dying of cancer."

"What's that?"

"Dying here."

"You've got a point," Dr. Croy said. "We start the first of the month."

PART ONE

1

The secretary, an olive-skinned beauty with a marked accent, opened the door and said, "You can come in now, Mr. Northrup."

Harry Northrup put aside a publication he had been skimming with restless eyes, a magazine published in the Caribbean Sea area which combined the maximum of abuse for the United States of America with a minimum of gratitude for her financial aid. He strode into an office overlooking the smokestacks of the great generating plant on the East River and let his eyes grow accustomed to the blaze of sunlight.

"Mr. Vyborg?"

Vyborg nodded. "Have a seat, Mr. Northrup," he replied in the hard gutturals of Scandinavia. "Can I help you?"

"Maybe."

Northrup studied the chief press officer of the United Nations. Soren Vyborg was a small-boned, fair-haired man in his early fifties with a foxy face and the bilious, blue eyes of the hard-pressed personnel of the great organization. He seemed neither happy, surprised, nor particularly interested in Northrup.

"Smoke?" Northrup asked.

"Thank you, never."

There was a moment of silence, and then Northrup said, "Have you been in touch with the press in the last several hours?"

Vyborg shook his head. "I've been attending the Assembly, Mr. Northrup. I just got back to my desk. I'm extremely busy." He made a delicate gesture of contained impatience. "I agreed to see you at your urgent request. Why?"

Northrup lit a cigar. "I'd like some information, Mr. Vyborg. Perhaps you might help me out."

"About what, Mr. Northrup?"

"This man."

Northrup opened a wallet and handed over an instant photograph of a white-haired man of dark skin. Even in death, force of character was expressed by the firm mouth, strong nostrils and powerful chin. The picture had been taken against the filth of a gutter somewhere in New York City. Bits of paper and a trickle of water flowed away from the head. Vyborg studied the head with interest.

"Why do you come to me?" he asked. "Why not to his own delegation?"

"I'm not sure who he is," Northrup replied. "But he is accredited to the United Nations?"

Vyborg carefully put the photograph aside. "Surely that did not require a personal visit?" he remarked, blowing smoke aside with a delicate hand. "But, yes! That is Carlos Pereira!" He mentioned a South American republic on the littoral of the Pacific—a country whose prosperity rested squarely on copper, tourism, agriculture of sorts, and guano dumped by millions of screaming sea birds which in turn prospered with the shifting vagaries of the Humboldt Current. Carlos Pereira had played a prominent role in recent debates concerning the delicate politics of a stormy continent. "But surely you knew?"

"Now I know," Harry Northrup said. "As of this moment, this man's identity was unknown."

"May I know the circumstances?"

"Oh, sure!"

Northrup stared at the blue sky beyond the greasy plumes of smoke arising from the great power plant in the East River. He was a short, stocky, powerful man with a broken nose and rugged features. The tenacity and alertness which had driven him to the command position of his own bureau in the Office of the District Attorney for New York County were evident.

"It's a bit baffling, Mr. Vyborg," he said carefully. "Early this morning, about 2 a.m., a patrol car of the 24th precinct was attracted to a location along the Hudson River near the boat basin." He described the asphalt pathway of Riverside Park where Pereira's body had been found, carelessly dumped behind a clump of bushes. The body had been stripped of all identification. A bullet had penetrated the head, bringing instant death. In the vicinity, torn bits of paper had been found, indicating credentials to the United Nations. It had seemed worth a call to the district attorney's office. Toward dawn, Harry Northrup had been roused from sleep and had driven to the scene of the crime.

"Is this all?" Vyborg asked finally.

"So far," Northrup said grimly. "Now that we've identified this man, we'll go farther. We're a bit touchy in New York County. We don't like our streets to be hunting grounds for those people to knock each other off. If Pereira had some trouble in his own country, let 'em settle it there."

"Can you be sure it was that sort of trouble?" Vyborg asked carefully.

"What sort?"

"You know," Vyborg suggested. "It might have been something of local origin. Carlos Pereira has been living in New York for ten years now. He has great power and influence in his own country, but he has been in virtual exile, as you must know. He has not been liked by his own government. It is conceivable that some difficulties may have arisen, but, on the other hand, he has been leading a full-blooded life in New York. Women, money, and—other activities might account for someone's desire to kill him."

Northrup was alerted by something in the other man's tone. He waited for the telephone to be answered and disposed of, and then put a question. "What other activities?"

Vyborg shrugged. "I must leave that sort of speculation to you, Mr. Northrup. Those of us attached to the Secretariat must be circumspect, but I would remind you that Mr. Pereira was attached to our committee in charge of settling the annual world production and distribution of narcotic drugs."

"Narcotics?" Northrup was instantly alerted. "Would you suggest that a man accredited to a U. N. delegation would be mixed up in that sort of thing?"

Vyborg smiled for the first time—a lacklustre cynical smile. "Oh, my dear Mr. Northrup," he said wearily. "Your kind of villainy is on a parochial scale indeed. You are lulled into all sorts of complacent illusions regarding our so-called statesmen, merely because you know your own breed. But these new nations? Where crime ends, politics begin! Slave traffic exists in some Arab states. Growing the poppy and trafficking in its derivatives is thoroughly moral in most of Asia. And I would not guarantee the blood-letting proclivities of some of our newer tribesmen. I am merely giving you a hint. The diplomatic pouch has been abused before. It may be again. And now, Mr. Northrup, I must ask specifically why you came to my office, and not to Mr. Pereira's! Really, I cannot believe that his identity was unknown when you came through that door."

"No," Northrup agreed. "I knew who he was. I didn't want to go directly to his own delegation."

"Why not?"

Northrup arose, surprisingly tall, considering his stocky shoulders. "A park officer spotted Pereira as one of a group of men who visited the *Balthazar* yesterday in the boat's tender."

The *Balthazar* was a medium-sized war vessel, destroyer class, anchored in the middle of the river.

Vyborg's glance was unwavering. "Has anything interesting been detected, Mr. Northrup?"

"Interesting? Its presence is interesting. A murder at a point facing its place of anchor is interesting. The busy activity of people coming and going is interesting. If you mean what's on that warship," Northrup smiled grimly, "that's another thing. It's a ship that has immunity."

"Ah? Immunity?" Vyborg found it useful to toy with a glass of water from a carafe. "Then of course your State Department should be alerted?"

"On what basis? That a man was knocked off in New York who might have paid that warship a visit? What would they do? Call Nasser for advice?" Northrup snorted with contempt and picked up his hat. "I'd like one favor, Mr. Vyborg."

"Yes?"

"I'd just as soon give this investigation a minimum of publicity. We'll get a play in the newspapers when we announce Pereira's identity, but I'd just as soon let your theory stand—some jealous husband, okay?"

"I'll be glad to oblige," said Vyborg with the foxy smile which, in the minds and hearts of men, had come to represent the great international organization.

The first afternoon newspapers were on the stands when Northrup left the United Nations Building and drove across

the city back to the park at the Hudson River. It was a
beautiful day in spring, warm and balmy, and the river was
blue and lovely, menacing only because of the blunt-nosed
grey warship at anchor in the river. The area staked out at
dawn by the Technical Services laboratory of the Police
Department had long since been picked clean of clues and
details, the body of Pereira had been removed to the City
Mortuary, and the only evidence of an investigation was a
heavy-set man in plainclothes eating bananas on a city bench.
He was reading the early editions as Northrup arrived.

"Message from the captain," Detective Dan Schreiber
mumbled through a stuffed mouth.

Northrup slumped on the bench. "What?"

Schreiber consulted a tattered notebook. "It seems like
this here Pereira was living on East 49th Street at the Whitman Hotel. They're rummaging now."

"Anything turn up?"

"Maybe."

Northrup stared at the privet hedges from which the body
had been recovered. The marks of heavy shoes in the grass
were still evident. A sweet smell pervaded the place of
death, but the busyness of the earlier scene had ended. "Let's
go," he agreed. "I'll drive."

The Governor Whitman Hotel was off Park Avenue, quiet
and sedate. It featured a cocktail lounge and a restaurant
alive with the chattering of television personnel and literary
agents telling each other genial lies. In its office, the manager, an eager man, was concluding an interrogation. Northrup entered quietly, and smoked with a menacing stare, until
the operation was concluded, and a report given in private.

"Now here's the thing," Captain Herman Collins, com-
manding officer of the Homicide Squad, Manhattan West,
recited, ticking off information on stubby fingers. "According to the manager, Pereira led a quiet life. He had a custom
of changing his girl friends every night, but that's respectable
by the standards of this here dump. Otherwise, a lot of rice
eaters used to come and go."

"Any Cubanos?"

"No." Collins grunted and went on. "Only visitors recently was this pack from South America. Here's a list of
names."

These names were immediately interesting. They were:

Francisco Morales Cruz (brother), Pascual Morales Perez (son), and Diego Morales Perez (son).

Northrup looked up. "Whose brother? Whose son?"

Captain Collins grinned smugly. "Juan Morales, El Benefactor!" He went on with evident enjoyment. "According to this manager, these three bums checked in last week. They got here in a 1961 Cadillac with DPL plates, and took separate suites on the fifth floor. A dozen minor guys are stashed away in odd places."

"They're not killing chickens in the bathtubs?"

"Hey? No! These are high guys in their country. They leave that to the cooks. Point is, they were having lots of visitors, especially Francisco—Uncle Francisco—and these visitors did not include their Ambassador to the United Nations or the New York Consul. It did include friend Carlos Pereira."

Northrup studied the list thoroughly. Suddenly he felt the hairs raise along his neck as if a cold wind were blowing, and there stood out, clear and stark, the vision of the warship in the harbor. He looked up grimly, "Any ideas, Captain?"

Captain Collins shook his head. "Not yet, but we got some questioning. What's on your mind?"

"How did these men get into the country? By plane?"

"No." Captain Collins lit a cigar. "They came by warship."

"The *Balthazar*?"

"It wasn't the *Lexington*." Captain Collins blew a plume of smoke. "Want me to round 'em up?"

Northrup shook his head. "No, not yet! If they've got diplomatic immunity, and maybe they have, maybe they haven't, questions wouldn't help. I want 'em kept under surveillance. I'd like to know what's on that warship."

"You got some way to get on, Mr. Northrup?"

"Maybe."

Northrup dropped the list of names into his wallet. "I'll let you know some more, Captain. Meanwhile, tell this manager if he breathes a word, we'll cut his ears off and close this dormitory. He's probably got cockroaches in the kitchen. Put a tracer on all these men—and, please—"

"Yeah?"

"If there's any tailing done, make sure your man goes ahead, not behind. I'd like to know whose goose the Morales boys are trying to cook."

"Will do!"

Captain Collins returned to the manager and barked orders while Northrup looked at his watch. Quarter past five. He could return to his office in the Criminal Courts Building. On the other hand, he had a plan of action, and other agreeable thoughts. He didn't have a time-clock to punch, but he was happiest when he was working late, till seven, eight, nine in the evening. Days like today left him feeling tense and jittery. He had accomplished nothing today. He didn't like that. He wanted to be in the midst of activity.

Picking up the phone, Northrup dialed a Plaza number, waited a moment, then said, "I'd like to talk to Miss Donna Reynolds, please. This is Harry Northrup."

A pause. Then the cool, poised voice of Donna said, "Hello, Harry. How's Mister D.A.?"

"Bored. How's Madison Avenue?"

"Yawning all over my gray flannel suit, Harry. Are you going to be finished down there in time for the opera?"

"Better news than that. I'm finished right now."

"What's the matter? Crime take a holiday?"

"Just one of those afternoons," Northrup said, vaguely. "I feel guilty walking out this early."

"I suppose you honestly do," Donna said levelly. "I wish I enjoyed my work the way you do."

"It isn't a matter of enjoying," Northrup said. He had tried to explain this before, without success. "Some people are born to spend their lives sweeping the streets. Others to play center field for the Yankees. Well, this is what I'm born to do. And I do it because I have to." He sighed. "To hell with the philosophy. As long as I'm through this early, what about dinner?"

"Early from what?"

"Investigation."

Donna teased, "Isn't this an honor? To interrupt your work for me?"

Northrup laughed. "Like the Fire Department. When you're waiting for a wall to fall, or a roof to crash, there's practically nothing to do but wait. It's up to the police now. What about Mama Pontaleone's?"

"Suits me," Donna said. "Meet you there?"

"Right. About six?"

Donna paused. "Can't. I've got to meet some prospects at the Plaza for cocktails. South American crowd. Don't drink till sundown."

Northrup paused. "South Americans?"

"Fascinating people," Donna said. "Don't you think?"

"Fascinating," Northrup agreed. "Make it eight." He hung up and arranged his thoughts. Donna was a good girl, he thought. Bachelor girl, with income, career and mind of her own. Ideal. Also the widest net of information of anyone he knew in the city. He arose and yawned, conscious that he had not slept the night before. Outside, Captain Collins was talking earnestly and menacingly to the unhappy manager of the hotel. The conversation was in Spanish.

Northrup came out. "Captain?"

Captain Collins cocked a grim and savage eye. "Yeah?"

"In the morning, I want autopsy reports, all DD-4's and 5's, and specific information on all contacts of the dead man and these Morales people. Okay?"

"You'll have it all," Captain Collins promised.

Northrup drove off in his souped-up 1955 Buick. It was the best his salary would allow, and he did not yet rate a city car of his own. He regretted missing the last presentation at the Met of *Don Giovanni*, but he could look forward to a spicy Italian dinner, a pleasant few hours with Donna, and who could tell where that might not lead?

2

La donna é mobile—

Donna Reynolds, the true Donna, smiled thinly and rather fondly at her stocky partner who was rubbing his broken nose with an air of abstraction. Mama Pontaleone's *ristorante* was good and cheap, just the place for a long comfortable talk over *chianti* and brandy. It was located in a converted brownstone house off Third Avenue and it provided home cooking—true home cooking—and supported all the Pontaleones: Mama, a vast, comfortable woman with a booming laugh and the shrewd good sense of a Milanese pawnbroker; Papa, a philosophical anarchist who sat hunched over the cashier's box, reading and re-reading a paperback edition of the Collected Works of Carlo Tresca; Betty, a sparkling student of political science at Hunter College who acted as waitress; Artie Levine, her fiancé, who cleared and washed dishes; nephews and nieces who came and went with the seasons; the other vague dependents whose laughter could be heard in the kitchen mingled with the wail of a small infant.

Just the place to relax lazily, hold hands, get drunk, and look forward to a comfortable night together in bed. It was sweet and domestic and cozy and Harry Northrup wasn't playing the game, she thought resentfully, not one bit. His gaze was inward, his thoughts were elsewhere. Irritatingly he was humming.

"Harry, darling," Donna said gently.

Northrup looked up. "Huh?"

"This Donna is going to be extremely *mobile* if she's not fed. Or has that fled from your mind?"

"Oh, sure!" Northrup was instantly contrite. He raised a finger and Mama Pontaleone came forward, all smiles and olive oil dimples. It was family style service—centerpiece of celery, radishes, olives, pickles, onions, *antipasto* to gratify a king; *zuppa, pasta,* roast lamb, *frutta,* coffee. In the grip of superior will power, Northrup, who had planned on nothing more weighty than *cannelone,* gave in with a sigh and let the riches of the kitchen come in a gratifying flood. He was good and amusing and made small talk, then lapsed again into his thoughts.

Donna took a cigarette. She smiled. "Darling?"

"Yeah?" Northrup said absently.

"How did you ever find Mama's place?"

"Why?"

"The food's so good. And Mama is so wonderful, and she makes this big city just a bit more like my little home town in Nebraska."

"Oh? This?" Northrup gazed about the wall with its portraits of Mazzini and Cavour and Garibaldi and a ribald caricature of Mussolini. "Most of the big racket men come here."

Donna's eyes widened. "Here? Why?"

"Custom," Northrup said briefly.

"What custom?"

"Oh, question of public relations."

Donna was instantly alert. "Tell me," she commanded, smiling into Northrup's level eyes. "This is my dish of tea."

Northrup struck a match and lit her cigarette. It was how the more important racket men managed to live in

the great city—making the rounds of public places, res-
taurants, bars, hotels, spending money freely, eating expen-
sively, displaying costly women, forming a milieu of sporting
life that spread across the country. It built respect and good
will and a grapevine of political connections that could
serve in good stead when it came to the appointment of
city and government officials.

Donna sat smoking. "Who are these people?" she wondered. "What sort are they?"

"Oh, people," Northrup said vaguely. "They're family
men—cruel to their enemies, brutal in their methods, cal-
lous to their casual women, but devoted in their own way
to family life and a code—"

Donna laughed. "Code?" she scoffed.

Northrup was not amused. "Yes, code," he agreed, and
lapsed again into his own thoughts. Donna patted a knuck-
led hand and studied a goblet of brandy, wondering at
her own patience with the powerful brute whose word
seemed her command. She had exhausted her own fund of
conversation describing a new situation in her line of work
—the representation of important hotel interests in India
which she was seeking to tie in with clients in Japan where
tremendous sums were being subscribed to build hotels for
the expected influx of tourists from the United States. It
was another fascinating world which kept her as intensely
absorbed in her work as Northrup was in his—

Yes, absorbed! she thought wistfully and a bit angrily.
At thirty-four Northrup was still a bachelor with no plans
to change that status. It was something she quite understood. He had been too busy rising out of the New York
public-school system and getting through Fordham Law
School. When one has gone to school by day and held
down jobs at night, one didn't look too soon for the career
handicap of marriage. By the time he was admitted to the
bar and finished with his military service and ready for his
quick rise through the hierachy and internal politics of the
district attorney's office, he had somewhere along the way
lost his interest in marriage. Temporarily, Donna hoped, sipping the good brandy of the mother country.

Donna had no illusions where she stood. She suited
Harry's needs at the moment. She was a good fellow, she
shared his toughness of mind; and she shared her bed with
him when the chance came, never raising sticky questions of

rings and altars. Sooner or later, she foresaw, some right guy would come along and propose a house in Scarsdale, and she would lose her taste or capacity to cope with Madison Avenue, and Harry Northrup would be confronted with a choice. And, no doubt, she mused dreamily, he would realize that true values and permanent happiness would lie only in the solid basis of family and home—

She shook herself angrily. At the moment Harry Northrup was paying less than no attention. He had gone back to Papa at the cashier's desk and picked up tomorrow morning's paper, which he was studying with intensity.

"What is it, Harry?" Donna asked.

Northrup said, "Case I was on today. You might be interested."

"Me? Why?"

"Something in your line," Northrup replied, handing over the paper. There was a photograph in the center piece of the dead man, Carlos Pereira, see story on page 2. Enterprising journalism had beat the police photographer to the scene. The privet hedge, the park bench, the river and the snout of *Balthazar* were all on display.

"Mine?" Donna was absorbed in the picture.

"You're still the P.R. girl for that banana republic?"

"Mm. What?" Donna looked up, interest and excitement dancing in her gray eyes. "It's not a banana republic. We— they, that is—import bananas from the same company you do. We go to mining."

"Anything else?"

Donna put aside the paper. "Such as?"

"Anything."

"What are you driving at?"

"I want some information on that alleged republic and some of its inhabitants."

Donna's gaze was frosty. "Harry Northrup," she said slowly, "are you asking me, a public relations woman, to breach the privileged and confidential relationship with a client?"

"I'm not asking about your retainer. Only about some of that country's citizens."

Donna felt a cold feeling at her heart. "Is that why you got me down here?" she demanded. "Why, good God, I would have spent the entire evening with a vulgar millionaire from Venezuela who showers girls with diamonds! Harry, am I being used by you?"

Northrup blinked. "Used?"

"I thought you had some feeling for me?" she said resentfully. "I thought this was a date."

"Well, it is!"

"Is it?" Donna stared. "Why? You can have me, body and soul, Harry Northrup, and all you want is information you can get out of the public library. Isn't that what you really want? Information?"

"Come on, darling!" Northrup protested. "Sure I love you, but just now I need some background, but not if you'll hate yourself in the morning. If you won't help, forget it!"

"No!"

Donna looked down at a tablecloth stained with marinara sauce, mentally cursing herself for allowing the mood to grow rancid. This was certainly not what she planned nor was it worthy of an organization woman. She forced a smile. "Is it so important, Harry?" she asked wonderingly.

"This man was murdered." Northrup said in a low voice. "I want the man who did it. When I get him I'll put him in the hot seat. I'll be there when it happens."

"Why? Is that the law?"

"No."

Donna paused. Then, "Is that necessary? That last touch?"

Northrup's eyes were level and disconcerting. "Murder gets me angry," he said. "It's my job to see that the right man pays off for it. I don't want the wrong man to burn. It's my own standard, to watch the finish, but it keeps me alert every minute of the way."

In the long pause the other couple paid their check and left the restaurant. Donna shivered at a side of this man she had never suspected. She said slowly, "It takes cruelty."

Northrup nodded. "Some. It's not a game."

Donna put aside her cigarette.

"Is love a game?" she asked. "Am I part of that game?"

Northrup hesitated. "No," he said slowly. "Love. Death. All part of life, and I love you."

Donna stared and then looked down, averting her gaze from his searching intensity. "Let's stop this," she said thickly. "I'm being a bore. Give me a moment." She sat with bowed head, breathing heavily, not hearing the sounds of the kitchen. She snapped open a compact and made up her lips. She forced a smile.

"If I refuse to give information?"

Northrup said lightly, "It might affect our sex life, darling."

Donna looked thoughtful. "I wouldn't want it to do that. Well, if my principles as a P.R. woman stand between me and my beloved, I'll have to yield, won't I? What's your question?"

Northrup placed the list of names before her. She studied the list carefully, ticking off information stored in a strong, retentive memory.

"Uncle Francisco is very nice," she advised. "Smooth. Loaded. Collects Modigliani paintings. Pascual does a terrific rumba and suffers from hay fever. Diego does deep-sea diving." She stopped.

"Yes?" He waited encouragingly.

"Juan Morales."

"El Benefactor?"

Donna looked up. "He's no benefactor," she smiled thinly, "He'd like to be. Commissioner of Internal Affairs today. Tomorrow the whole country!"

"Really?"

"Really!" Donna described cocktails with the silver-haired statesman on the S. S. *Bolivar,* a South American cruise, which had led to the retainer for representation of various hotel interests in that continent. Morales—Juan Morales— had suave and continental manners, a flood of dialectical observations on the decline of capitalism as a solution to world problems, and almost pure Incan blood, reflected in coppery skin, piercing eyes and an air of timeless planning. Behind him lay turbulent years of political strife marked by refuge taken in the Bolivian Embassy, years of exile in Switzerland, enigmatic travels to the Far East, and an uneasy truce between his party and that of the aged general whose arthritic hands were gradually loosening their control of the reins of power.

"Does any of this help?" Donna asked.

"Not particularly," Northrup said with dissatisfaction. "There must be something more cooking. What does the Commissioner of Internal Affairs mostly do?"

"He waits."

"Waits for what?"

"He waits for El Presidente to be gathered to his fathers. Incan civilization rested on the patience of its subjects. So does Morales."

"Ah? And while waiting?"

Donna was powdering a pretty nose. Over the compact mirror her gaze was level. "He administers the really lucrative business of the country. Next after copper and tin."

"What's that?"

Donna snapped the compact shut. "The coca leaf," she said briefly. "The only thing that makes life in that country worthwhile. Let's call it a night, darling."

"Hey, what?"

Donna rose. "Your mind isn't on me," she observed. "It's elsewhere, isn't it?"

Northrup shrugged and called for Mama Pontaleone and the check. "Well, maybe. I'm wondering about the *Balthazar*. Would there be any way to arrange for me to get on for a look-see?"

A jaunty bit of millinery was placed on a gorgeous pile of hair. Donna smiled thinly and measured the grim, rugged features across the tablecloth. Now why, she wondered wistfully, had she ever allowed her heart to be so taken by the brute? "You're a big boy, Harry," she said lightly, patting his wrist, "and business is business. Let me think about it."

Which was her way of saying, File and forget! Northrup managed to lead Donna out past the good wishes and cordiality of the entire Pontaleone family and led her to his car. He drove up Third Avenue to Donna's apartment on East 56th Street, an expensive trap complete with centralized air conditioning, low ceilings, thin walls, terrace, and a view of the United Nations Building looming over the East River.

"I'll come up," Northrup said.

Donna was silent as he pressed the elevator button. The mood was angry and disturbed. At her door, she turned as he embraced her and kissed her neck and hair and finally her passive mouth.

"Can I come in?" he asked. "I'm sorry I spoiled your evening, but I'd like to make it up?" He sniffed her hair. "You smell so good."

Donna smiled crookedly. "Good night, Harry," she said briefly. "That elevator has a cybernetic control system. It's waiting. You mustn't disappoint a thinking machine. It has feelings too." She rose on her toes and kissed him.

"It's all right, Harry, my darling," she said lightly, and disappeared into her apartment.

It was after two when Northrup eased into a parking spot at the hydrant in front of a reconverted brownstone in the East Thirties. He walked up three flights and entered an unpretentious two-room flat which showed Donna's good taste as a decorator. He found milk and apple pie in the refrigerator and sat down to the end of the Late, Late Show on television—a crime picture that revolted his professional sense—and he was left alone with his thoughts, not the most pleasant in the world, he was sure.

He had barely fallen asleep when the telephone rang.

A deep voice growled. "Mr. Nort'rup? Schreiber here."

Northrup scratched his head. "You know what the hell time it is?"

"Sure! Time for all good men to come to the aid of the party." Schreiber laughed immoderately. "I also got some news. The captain thought you might want this. Pereira case."

Northrup was instantly alert. "What about that?"

Schreiber chuckled provocatively. "I got some notes here in my little black book—"

"Never mind those notes. What's the news?"

"These men? I followed them—"

"What men?"

"I don't mean Wynken, Blynken and Nod," Schreiber said good-humoredly. "I mean Francisco, Pascual and Diego. For a couple of visiting firemen, they' been lurking around in funny places. Such as Brooklyn."

"Brooklyn?"

"The proud borough," Schreiber added informatively. He waited, and went on. "Especially Diego. Man he met is one Carl Malfino."

"Malfino?"

"Know the name?"

"Oh, sure!"

Northrup was conscious of a dripping faucet in the kitchenette. "Now, why," he said slowly, "why would three *caballeros* come eight thousand miles to Brooklyn to meet a bum like Carl Malfino?"

"I wouldn't know," said Schreiber cheerfully, and there was a sound of teeth being picked and sucked of shreds of frankfurter and a swelling belch that told of beer and sauerkraut consumed in the dead of night. "It ain't to crochet."

"That's a reasonable conclusion," Northrup admitted. He had in mind a youth sent up several years earlier to Dannemora for armed robbery. Occasionally his name had come up in what passed for conversation at Dino's Restaurant on Mulberry Street—the shop talk of prosecutors and parole officers. What brought his name instantly to attention was the family firm name—Paul Malfino, Sr., Gravel and Sand. Newspapers. Imports and Exports. Respectability plus! And a mother of South American stock. "Any ideas?"

"Nope." Schreiber added hopefully. "I could make a collar and ask?"

Northrup looked at his watch. Quarter past five. Everything seemed to happen at a quarter past five! "Tell Captain Collins to keep a tail on all those bums," he suggested. Ten minutes later he was asleep.

Three hours later Northrup was at his desk in the Criminal Courts Building. At the coffee break, Schreiber called back, hoarse and weary.

"Malfino left this morning," Schreiber boomed.

"Left?" Northrup drummed the desk top. "For where? Mars?"

"Dannemora."

Schreiber waited for effect. "I followed him to Grand Central. According to the ticket seller, he picked up a ticket that takes him to Plattsburg. If you want, I can catch a plane and head him off? But frankly, that sack looks good to me."

Northrup considered a pile of legal documents on his desk. "Don't bother," he said slowly. "We've got to be logical, Dan. Right?"

"Right!" Schreiber said fervently.

"We've got to assume some connection between yesterday's meeting with Diego Morales and today's trip to Dannemora?"

"No question!"

"In that case, something smelly is going on?"

"Smelly, indeed!"

"Then let's turn over no garbage cans until they're full,"

Northrup advised. "Pick up again with Malfino when he gets back to New York."

"Good enough," Schreiber said, incuriously, he yawned and hung up.

Northrup waited a moment and requested a familiar number at a nearby office.

"State Parole Commission," a bored voice answered. Moments later Northrup was talking to State Parole officer Dominick Maestroangeli.

"Yes, Mr. Northrup?" Maestroangeli asked in respectful, adenoidal tones. "How can I help?"

"You've got a file on a man named Carl Malfino?"

A pause.

"Why, sure," Maestroangeli answered cautiously. "Why?"

"Did you know he left the city this morning?"

Maestroangeli retreated further into caution. "Of course I know. He wanted permission to go to Dannemora."

"What the hell for?"

"Personal business," Maestroangeli said. "He went to visit a friend of the family. Scarpa."

Northrup waited.

"Baldo Scarpa?"

"Why, yes!" Maestroangeli said. "Know him?"

"A bit," Northrup said heavily. "He had something to do with undermining Prohibition. He's been at Dannemora since before you started to shave."

"I remember," Maestroangeli replied.

"What made you let Malfino go, eh?"

"He made a good case," Maestroangeli said in troubled tones. "Don't you know about Scarpa?"

"Know what?"

Maestroangeli described the cancer experiment to which Baldo Scarpa had subjected himself. "According to Carl, his daughter is terribly concerned—"

"Daughter?"

"Helen. Married, with a small kid, so she can't go herself. She's worried about the old man—"

"So Carl gets permission to visit?"

"Why, yes!" Maestroangeli said uneasily. "Carl's been keeping his nose clean. It seems logical. And Scarpa seems entitled to a visit from the family under the circumstances. I'm not sticking my neck out, am I? I mean, you haven't got anything on Carl I don't know about?"

"No, no!" Northrup grunted. "Just on a list of names I'm tabbing. Keep me posted from now on, eh?"

"Anything you say, Mr. Northrup."

Northrup hung up. To let Malfino, a man on parole from a conviction for armed robbery out on a string that would lead into the big prison at Dannemora! What was the parole officer thinking? It came from being swamped—Dom Maestroangeli, B.A., M.A., candidate for M.S.W. at the New School for Social Work, father of five, graduate of the Educational Alliance, one of less than one hundred and fifty exhausted parole officers looking after the health, wealth and sex life of more than seven thousand conniving parolees! What could anyone expect?

Northrup lit a rank cigar and swiveled, staring moodily at the City Prison looming across the areaway. Some advantage might be found by fishing in muddy waters. Suddenly the pattern of glass block windows took the form of a chess board. A pawn had been advanced. Perhaps.

Northrup picked up his phone and dialed an interoffice number. "Get me all you can on Baldo Scarpa," he said crisply. He spelled the last name. "He's at Clinton. Long-term man. Kidnapping, I think. Been there since around, oh, maybe '43 or '44. One of the war years." Switching over to another line, he said to the switchboard girl, "Get me long distance, honey. I want to talk to Lee Brian, Clinton Prison, Dannemora, New York."

Time passed. Other calls came in. Northrup signed forms and shoved them aside. Then the switchboard girl's voice said, "I have the party you requested, Mr. Northrup."

"Hello?" a gruff, distant voice said. "Northrup?"

"Lee. Listen, I want you to do me a favor," Northrup said, without preamble. Brian was a busy man, with a swarming prison of incorrigibles to take care of. He didn't have time for pleasantries about the weather.

"What kind of favor?"

"You remember Carl Malfino?"

"Armed robbery. Paroled around a year or so ago."

"That's the one. Well, he's on a train right now, heading up to see you. Sort of an alumnus coming to visit the old school."

"What the hell?"

"That was my reaction. But the parole officer let him go," Northrup said.

"Let him go?" Brian said incredulously. "Did he read the psychiatric evaluations?"

"What evaluations?"

"Projective tests!" Brian said grimly. "Malfino's a psychopath. Not enough to send him to Mattewan, but enough to make him real dangerous. Character disorder. Amoral. Assaultive, paranoid, but good compensating devices. And smart. I'll put him on a train right back. What is this? A mountain resort?"

"He's coming up to see Baldo Scarpa. I imagine Scarpa's entitled to a visitor?"

"Not an ex-inmate."

"It must have been fixed up."

"I'll unfix!"

"No."

"What?"

"I want him to see the old man."

Brian hesitated. "The rules, Harry—"

"Bend 'em. What will it cost the state to bug the room?"

"Oh."

"Yes, oh!"

Brian chuckled suddenly. "Can I serve 'em a steak dinner? It's open house up here and I get lonely for good conversation. Okay, Harry. Only don't let 'em know at the New York *Post*. Last time they had a writer up here, we all suffered. Will do!"

Northrup thanked the prison man and broke the connection. He felt a surge of excitement. Someone had taken a step that might lead to a solution of the blankness that surrounded the Pereira case. A tap on the door brought a messenger with DD-4's and DD-5's—the reports of the Detective Division on the fruitless investigation that turned up nothing except the history of a functionary of a foreign government who lived a full-blooded life in a city of attractive women and opportunities for personal diversions— nothing beyond the routine surroundings of a gun killing in the city of New York. No witnesses, no clues, no weapon. Nothing but the location, and the enigmatic association with three visitors from another continent. The autopsy report of the Medical Examiner's Office showed nothing that Harry Northrup might not have surmised. The only surprise was an enlarged heart, dental caries, and the scar tissue of a prostate operation—none of which accounted for death as satisfactorily as the pellet of lead that had plowed through bone and brain tissue, bringing instant death. Powder marks showed that the gun, a .45 Luger, had been pressed against the base of the skull at the moment of firing.

Scarpa? Why Scarpa?

That would develop in time, Northrup thought. At least something was in motion now. And then the file on Baldo Scarpa arrived.

Scarpa was 67 years old. Born in Sicily, arrived in the United States at Galveston in 1912, citizenship granted in the United States District Court for the Southern District of New York in 1919. Rejected for military service World War I for record of petty offenses. Married 1922. Son born 1923, killed in the Pacific 1943. Daughter, Helen, born 1931, only surviving child. Helen married 1955.

Sentenced to five years in 1924 for extortion. Paroled 1927. Sentenced to eight years for manslaughter in 1932. Paroled 1938. Sentenced in 1943 for kidnapping—

Kidnapping?

Northrup turned a page and committed to memory an involved case dealing with the official owner of a distillery whose real owner seemingly was Baldo Scarpa. Sentence imposed by Judge Wallace. Twenty-five years to life. This time Baldo Scarpa had not been lucky. Seventeen years at Dannemora on the last fall, and parole applications turned down annually. He was on ice, it would seem, for the rest of his life.

Extortion, manslaughter, kidnapping—not a pretty customer, Northrup thought. He stared at a twenty-year-old photograph. It showed a lean, almost cadaverously gaunt man of middle years with deep-set eyes staring savagely out of heavy bony sockets. Thick black eyebrows formed two fierce slashes across a corrugated forehead. His nose was sharply hooked, lips thin, chin bold and prominent. There was a look of strength—of immense force in reserve, force, and sullen hatred. Northrup wondered what seventeen years in Clinton Prison had done to that face—whether they had sharpened the blazing intensity of those eyes, the cruel curve of the lips. What undetected acts of violence lay behind those black depths?

What was Malfino's interest in the old man? What had the parole officer said? Malfino and Scarpa's daughter? But that was years ago, because the daughter—what was her name? Helen—Helen Scarpa had been married for some years now. Or had Scarpa sent for Malfino? The annual application for parole? In that case, why had a lawyer not been sent for?

Scarpa!

Northrup found himself staring with fascination. Scarpa had been out of circulation for years. He had no current rating. He was somebody out of the distant past. Kids who hadn't reached puberty when Scarpa was put away for the third time now were big shots in East Coast crime. Anyway, Scarpa wasn't coming out of Dannemora for a good many more years, if ever. Malfino might have gone up there on purely social motives, Northrup thought sickly.

No. That didn't make sense.

Northrup shoved the Scarpa file into his desk and put in a phone call to the Hotel Whitman, where he had one of his detectives, Bill Duyckman, sitting in a fifth-floor room watching the Morales delegation.

"Anything?" Northrup asked hopefully.

"Quiet day," Duyckman reported. "Old Morales hasn't left his suite yet. He had two visitors this morning."

"You find out who?"

"One was a Brazilian, I guess. He was speaking Portuguese in the elevator, anyway. The other I couldn't find anything out about. Rodriguez says he had an Argentinian accent."

"Any luck with the chambermaids?"

"Some," Duyckman said. "I planted a mike in the suite the two Morales sons have. But there's no hope of getting a bug on the uncle if he never leaves the suite."

"Keep at it," Northrup said. He dropped the phone back into its cradle. This operation was keeping men tied up doing nothing. Watch and wait. Watch Malfino. Watch the hotel. Watch the ship. And wait.

The telephone jangled.

Tiredly. "Yes?"

Maestroangeli sounded pleased. "Something on Malfino!"

Northrup pulled over a scratch pad. "Let's have it."

"This squeal comes from Brooklyn. Malfino's been eating lunch in this place around Flatbush Avenue and Fulton—"

"So Malfino eats lunch," Northrup grunted.

The parole officer paused, hurt. "Will you wait, Mr. Northrup?" he complained. "Do you want this, or not?"

"Not by way of the North Pole. Don't give me the menu."

A coughing spell, then a strangled voice came back. "Sure, Mr. Northrup! Sorry, but with this case load of bums, I'm eating my lunch and it went down the wrong way." A throat was cleared. "Pastrami," Maestroangeli explained, and went on to advise that a Brooklyn detective had identified the luncheon companion of Malfino as a man whose picture that day in the *News* was that of a man named Perez—

"Morales Perez," Northrup corrected, instantly alert, and splinters of a pencil lay strewn. "Diego Morales—and forget the Perez part. That's the mother's name. I know all about it."

A moment of reproachful silence. "Jeez, Mr. Northrup! What is this? A one-way street? Don't I get to know too? How does it look for the record, I mean? Oh, this is nice!"

Patience and fortitude! Northrup thought, invoking the motto of the city. Aloud he said, "It was an accident, Dom. I was watching our friend Diego and the delegation."

"Oh!" the parole officer said intelligently. "You mean, somebody might want to knock 'em off?"

"I'm watching them," Northrup said without spelling it out. "And it happened that I got word about lunch with Malfino. So I learned Malfino was leaving the city. Routine."

"Can you tell me what's up?"

Northrup sighed. "I'd love to, Dom," he said with an air of sincerity. "Let me work on it. I'll let you know."

The telephone was reproachfully silent.

"Gee, Mr. Northrup! This thing can look very bad for me," the parole officer complained. "Nobody tells me my man is lunching with these foreign bums. I'm trying to create a good working relationship with my men. Mutual confidence. Interpersonal relationships. You know, environment has so much to do with this structuring of personality difficulties—all that crap! But for crissake! I can't be every place—"

"All right, Dom," Northrup said.

"Mr. Northrup, I'm writing this master's thesis—"

"Yes, Dom!"

"If he steps out of line, I swear I'll personally kick the guts out of him—"

"Dom—"

"I'm trying to show these bums how to act like men—"

Northrup broke in. "Dom, I'm terribly sorry, but my other phone is ringing! I'll be in touch—"

Maestroangeli went on excitedly. "One wrong move, and this son of a bitch goes back to the can! Why should I stick my neck out? Why—"

"Shut up!"

"Huh?" The parole officer came to a halt.

Northrup spelled it out carefully. "Dom, I'll take full responsibility if anything goes wrong. I don't want Malfino back in the can."

"You're sure?"

"Not till I let you know. If things work out, you'll get a letter of commendation from the district attorney himself. From my boss to yours. Now that's a promise. With a copy to your professor."

A pause. "Can I depend on that? I'd like it in writing."

Northrup appreciated a nice point and made one himself. "Have I ever let you down, Dom?" he asked sweetly.

"No, but—"

"You have my word as a lawyer," said Northrup with the warmth and sincerity that came from years of training and discipline in the art of persuading juries to bring in verdicts for the prosecution. He placed his hand on Gilbert's Code of New York Criminal Procedure. "My solemn word!"

"Well—"

Maestroangeli hesitated, and agreed, and it was a settled matter. Northrup swung around, smoking his cigar, rubbing the back of his neck, grimly wondering just whose neck was out. At the moment, Carl Malfino was on a train rattling its way to the Adirondacks. Warm days and cool nights. Fish in icy streams, deer bounding across roads, browsing in the hazy forests, a grim, stone house on a hill and a fierce, caged animal prowling a confined space and gazing out to a sky of freedom.

He threw away a cold cigar and went back to work. In the long run, it might lead back to the man, or men, who ordered Carlos Pereira, diplomat, politico, bon vivant, to be killed.

3

Two days passed. The weather turned warm, and Northrup was grateful for the blessing. Joe Scott, another of the assistant

district attorneys, came down with appendicitis, and Northrup found himself with the tail end of a group of witnesses
in a numbers racket investigation Scott had prepared for the
grand jury. Plans to see Donna that Thursday night fell
through, and instead of a Swedish movie, they settled for a
quick coffee in midtown. They made plans for a show on
the weekend, if nothing came up before.

"What could come up?" Donna asked.

"I'm not sure."

Friday morning, Northrup finished presenting his witnesses
to the grand jury and spent a gabby half-hour on the
telephone with Scott at the hospital, describing his difficulties,
and planning the presentation of a sealed indictment for maximum surprise in a series of planned raids. Northrup did not
mind the extra load. With the Pereira case in suspension,
he was glad to be occupied. He toyed dimly with the notion
of invading the *Balthazar*—a notion he dropped. He could
hardly board the ship under circumstances which would pre-
clude action even by Federal authorities. The fear of screams
of Latin rage, it seemed, controlled American authorities
on all levels.

Maestroangeli called.

"Malfino's back," the parole officer said with relief. "The
son of a bitch just called from the station. He's heading for
home. He'll be here Monday for his regular visit. Oh, jeez,
is that a load off my mind! I didn't sleep for three nights."
A heavy sigh floated over the wire.

Northrup was not impressed. He had his own sleepless
nights. "What's his schedule?"

"Once a month."

"Is that enough?"

Maestroangeli's voice rose defensively in complaint. "Make
up your mind, Mr. Northrup! Which way am I supposed to
play with the man? On the record, he's keeping his nose
clean since he got out. Once a month's all he needs to
come in. The guy's got a job, you know."

"Doing what?"

"He's an assistant sexton at the Church of the Holy Name
on Flatbush Avenue."

Northrup's eyebrows rose. *"Malfino?"*

"His father's been a big contributor to the church charities
over the years, and so they took him in. Redemption
of the sinful, you know. He gets about forty bucks a week

sweeping the place out and tending the garden." Maestro-angeli chuckled, feeling better.

Northrup tried to picture that cold, harsh, deadly man sweeping the floor of a church. He failed utterly. It was easier to think of an axe-murderer taking up knitting.

"You figure he's going to make a career out of it?" North-rup asked.

"He's talking about entering the priesthood. This is just the first step on the path."

"Dom, you're a Catholic. Would *you* want to get spiritual advice from somebody like Carl Malfino?"

Maestroangeli laughed. "Oh, they wouldn't give him any important position, because of his record. They'd send him off to Africa as a missionary. That's what's usually done in such cases. And maybe thirty years from now they'd let him come home and live in one of the local parishes. He might never become a priest. Just stay a deacon and help out."

Northrup said quietly, "Couldn't he be conning?"

"Oh, sure!" Maestroangeli sounded better, now on familiar territory. "But why go behind the record? What else have I got to go by? And I sure feel better with a priest looking after the man than some Joe Hood in the garment center. Maybe some of this can rub off—who knows? Last visit, he didn't talk anything but church history. He was quoting some authority named Guignebert—"

"A Frenchman?"

"Yeah. I had him spell it out. Guignebert is some big authority—why?"

Northrup grunted. "Guingnebert is anti-Church!" he said sardonically. "Didn't you know?"

"Jeez, no! I don't read that stuff."

"I did, and I caught hell from my professor at Fordham! It got me an F once in a course." Northrup paused. "It's heavy reading. Maybe Malfino has got more on the ball than he lets anyone see."

Maestroangeli sounded subdued. "How do you like that?" he marvelled. "The guy had me going. Still," he added hopefully, "maybe, just maybe, this job is working on the personality structure of the bastard. Maybe there's a missing super-ego—"

Northrup held the clacking hearing piece to his ear while he made notes on a yellow pad, occasionally grunting to show attention. Somewhere along the line he broke in blind.

"We've got to watch him though, Dom," he advised. "He's a convict on parole, let's not forget."

"I'm not forgetting it. Have a good weekend."

"You, too!"

Hanging up, Northrup repressed a grim chuckle. Malfino sweeping church floors. Malfino a possible missionary! Where? To Cuba? Or some other country in South America? Well, well! He turned about and selected a file from an array stacked behind him across the window sill and pulled out an old report going back to Malfino's conviction for armed robbery—reduced to a lesser charge on a plea of guilty.

Assaultive personality, repressive structure, residues of feeling, grandiose conception—

Clinical jargon, but the psychiatric report attached to the probation officer's recommendations to the court had described anything but a personality suited to a turned-around collar. Northrup thought back to a coldly feral look on the subject's face at the moment of sentence some years back.

The afternoon moved along. At closing time, the docket seemed clear, leaving the week free. But then a clerk entered with a flat package plastered with special delivery stamps. It was the tape requested from Dannemora—the tape of Carl Malfino's bugged conversation with Baldo Scarpa! A current of nervous excitement made the muscles of Northrup's left cheek throb suddenly.

He signed quickly for the tape and closed his office door. It was too late in the day to bring a stenographer in, but that didn't really matter. He didn't expect to find anything of permanent value on the tape. Just a hint, he prayed silently. Just a smidgeon of an indication of how Malfino—and Scarpa—could be linked to the Pereira case. On Monday he could make a transcript for the records.

Northrup hauled his tape recorder out of the cabinet and plugged it in. Quickly prying the tape out of its wrapper, he threaded it through the playback heads and attached its lead end to the empty spool. Moistening his lips tensely, he turned the knob to *PB* and sat down on his green leather couch to listen.

Three or four minutes of silence. They had begun recording too soon.

Then a cough. A door opening, closing.

A flat official voice said, "Okay, Malfino. You've got fifteen minutes. I'll be waiting right outside."

"Thanks very much, officer. I really appreciate this." That was Malfino's voice, deep and harsh, but cultured and educated-sounding.

"Don't thank me. Thank old man Brian. I wish I knew how you rated this."

Door sounds again.

Then Malfino's voice. "Baldo. Baldo. How's it been going?"

"I get along." A high-pitched, reedy, heavily accented voice. "Good to see you, Carl."

"Good to see you. You're looking swell."

"That isn't true. I am an old man, Carl."

"Come off it! You don't look a day over fifty!"

"Did you come all the way up here to tell me lies?" Scarpa asked without rancor.

"I came to tell you that I saw Helen, and she's fine. Also the kid. Tommy. He's five, and big as an eight-year-old. A great kid."

"I hope to see him someday."

"Sure you will, Baldo."

"And the husband? This Irish? Is he well too?"

"He's okay. A nice guy. Not much to him, but a nice guy. I think Helen's happy with him."

"You only *think*?" Baldo said edgily. "I want my daughter to be happy! And my grandson!"

"I tell you they're getting along fine, Baldo. And I got regards for you from a lot of old friends. Pat Macaluso. Danny Chiara. Leo Monte. Sal Arcidiacono. They all send their best. They want to know when you're gonna come out of this dump and see them and say hello."

"You are on parole, Carl. You know you should not be seeing such men!"

"Baldo, Baldo, you'll never guess how I see them!"

"How?"

"In church! I work at Holy Name. I help the sexton out. I sweep the floors, I put the prayer books back in the racks, I mow the lawns. And they come to the church. That's how I see them."

"You work in church, Carl?"

"It's about time I did something decent, no?"

"And you see Sal and Leo and Danny and Pat. Tell them hello for me. But when I get out of here I do not want to see them again."

"How's that, Baldo?"

"You heard me. Do you know how many years of my
life I have spent in jails, Carl? Twenty-six years! That is a
great many. My son Nick lived only twenty years his whole
life, and here I have spent twenty-six in prisons! It is enough.
It is more than enough. Baldo Scarpa wants nothing to do
with his old life."

A pause.

Malfino said, "You're just going to snub all your old
friends when you get out, Baldo?"

Scarpa sighed. "I want to settle down with my daughter and get to know her. She was only a child when I went
away. Now she is a woman, a mother."

"But you could still be a big man, Baldo!"

"Are you trying to tempt me with something?"

"Me? I'm going straight, Baldo. I'm not getting mixed up in
anything! Just because I see some of the boys at the
church, it don't mean—"

"The old days were great," Baldo mused suddenly. "You
were nothing then. A runny-nosed brat. 1925, 1930—I was a
big man then! Baldo Scarpa! Mothers used to scare the kids
with my name! And now look. An old man. My hands shake.
My hair is white. The past is past, Carl. What few years I
have left, I will spend quietly."

"So you're figuring on getting out of here pretty soon,
Baldo?"

"There is a chance. There is a chance."

"Will you come around to the church when you get out?"

"I want no trouble, Carl. I can't afford it. I'm a three-
time loser already. One more conviction and I never see freedom again."

"I tell you, Baldo, I'm not mixed up in anything. I just
work at the church."

"Sure. Sure, Carl."

"Your time's up," a voice called.

"Well, it was good seeing you, Baldo."

"I'm glad they let you talk to me, Carl."

"So am I, Baldo. Stay well."

"Stay well, Carl."

The sound of a door.

Then silence.

Northrup remained seated, letting the rest of the tape
run out, while his mind went over the details of the conversation he had just heard. The flapping end of the tape

brought him out of his reverie. Crossing the room to the tape recorder, he switched it off, rethreaded the tape, rewound it, and played it through from the beginning, listening now for the key phrases his mind had seized upon, and trying to read their true meanings from minute turns of inflection.

I got regards for you from a lot of old friends.

But when I get out of here I do not want to see them again.

You're just going to snub all your old friends when you get out, Baldo?

I want to settle down.

But you could still be a big man, Baldo!

Are you trying to tempt me with something?

Me? I'm going straight, Baldo.

Northrup heard the tape through to the finish, then shut the machine off. Removing the tape, he restored it to its container and locked it away carefully. Not that there was anything very important in it. Malfino had been well aware that any words he spoke to the old man within the prison walls would be monitored and probably recorded. But the conversation held oblique hints and suggestions. And, of course, Northrup knew nothing of the gestures and facial expressions that went with the words. The winks, the frowns, the grins.

Malfino was up to something. That went almost without saying. Malfino wouldn't have made the long, dreary train journey to Dannemora just to say hello to an old family friend. No, it had been a kite-flying expedition, Northrup was positive.

And Baldo. The three-time loser eager to settle down in his declining days. How sincere was that? Did he really mean it, or was that just a pious wish uttered for public consumption, when what he really wanted to do was reassume his old underworld importance?

Hard to tell without talking to Scarpa himself, Northrup thought.

He went over and over the conversation. Malfino was using his church job as a means of getting around the parole restrictions, obviously. He was seeing men like Monte and Macaluso, remnants of Baldo's old gang. They were men in their fifties and sixties now, but they were still powers in New York gangdom. Northrup smiled at Malfino's cleverness. Who would suspect a man who left Dannemora to take a humble job as a church sexton? Certainly not a naive, hopeful man like Dom Maestroangeli. And if a Macaluso or an Arcidiacono decided to drop around to church some quiet afternoon and have a couple of casual words with the sexton's assistant, who could suspect skulduggery?

Things began to take shape in Northrup's mind. Malfino was setting up a deal for that South American crowd. But he needed Scarpa, for some reason. Only old Baldo was reluctant to risk trouble, now that he stood on the verge of release from prison. Malfino had extended a cautious feeler to Scarpa, and—ostensibly, at least—had been rebuffed. But who could be sure? Who knew what really passed between those two men, beneath the surface of their mere words?

A visit to Dannemora might be in order, Northrup decided. He could learn more from a face-to-face confrontation with old Scarpa than by listening to his taped conversation. Northrup hated this stage of an investigation, this shadow-boxing with no tangible opponent. But it was necessary, he told himself. Prosecuting a case didn't mean only bang-bang action and clear-cut arrests. There were long days of lying in wait, of sniffing around the edges of a case, of marking time. An impatient man, Northrup loathed such days. But he had to put up with them.

He checked the time. Half past six on a Friday afternoon. The Criminal Courts Building was clearing out rapidly, hardly anyone still hanging around. Northrup paused out in front, looking out across the little park at the formal majesty of the buildings ringing the district. The air was still warm from the foretaste of summer that had brushed the city earlier in the day. Tiny yellowish buds were beginning to sprout belatedly on the maple trees.

Brooklyn-bound traffic moved busily past him, heading for the bridges. The city was busy. The city throbbed with life and vitality.

Fridays depressed him. He felt tired and empty and alone. Crossing Foley Square, Northrup went into a bar on the far side of Centre Street and nodded wearily at the bald, cheerful barkeep.

"Tough day, Mr. Northrup?"

"They're all tough days, Johnny. Let me have a beer, will you?"

Northrup didn't drink tap beer. The barkeep knelt and drew a bottle of Heineken's out of the refrigerator below the counter. He uncapped it and poured it carefully into a glass. Northrup didn't like a head on his beer, either. He put a dollar down on the counter and picked up the glass.

The place was almost empty. The barkeep leaned forward confidentially and said, "I hear that rape case went to the jury today, Mr. Northrup. The guy who raped the colored girl in Greenwich Village."

"Did it?" Northrup smiled absently. "Not my department."

"I thought maybe it was. Jeez, I hope they throw the book at that guy. Imagine, a nice sweet kid of sixteen, and he has to do a thing like that to her. You just got to look at the guy's picture and you know he's guilty. You ask me, that sort ought to be taken out and shot."

Northrup made no reply. He knew the case. A messy deal. Fellow picked out of a lineup by a hysterical girl and a none too reliable witness. Northrup had talked to the man prosecuting, Shel Weintraub. Weintraub had a couple of private doubts about the man's guilt, at least in this particular instance. That he was a perverted psychopath, nobody doubted seriously. But that he had committed the particular crime for which he had been arraigned and indicted—

"What's the matter, Mr. Northrup? I say something out of line?" the bartender wanted to know.

"No, Johnny. Nothing you said. Sorry."

"Don't you think the guy's guilty?"

"Not my case," Northrup said. He took the sting off his curt reply with a smile, and finished his beer. "See you Monday, Johnny."

"Have a good weekend, Mr. Northrup."

"Thanks," the assistant district attorney said. "You too, Johnny."

Northrup left and headed quickly for his car. Would the end of the road lead to the solution of the homicide in Riverside Park?

4

It was a long evening. Donna had a date, and Northrup had failed to make other arrangements. Thrown back on his own resources, he ate alone in a Spanish restaurant near his apartment. He walked the neighborhood until it was dark and then went home.

It was not often that he had an evening to himself and in his more hectic moments he longed for just such a night. But now he was uneasy and restless. He could play his records, read a book, mix daiquiris and relax. But not tonight. He kept thinking of the *Balthazar*, lying at anchor in the river, perhaps holding the secret of the dead man found in the park.

The case refused to leave his mind. It nagged him. It would be an intolerable weekend, he saw.

He went to bed early and had a hard time falling asleep. When slumber came, it was shallow and intermittent, courtroom scenes mingling with the sight of a dead man, and when he woke for good, around six the next morning, he struggled out of a dream in which he was making a violent and angry summation to the jury sitting on the trial of the murderer of a man named Pereira.

Only who was the murderer?

He struggled to retain the dream and then he found himself sitting up, tired and more despondent than when he had gone to bed.

He frittered away the hours until ten before he dialed a familiar number. The phone rang five times, and he was about to hang up when a sleepy voice said, "Um. Hello?"

"This is Harry. I wake you?"

"Uh. Sort of." A yawn sounded delightfully. "You sound funny, darling?"

Northrup paused. "You took a long time answering."

"So I did," Donna said equably. "Why?"

"For a moment, I wondered whether you got home last night."

"Why, my darling!" Donna said with delight. "Now you sound jealous and competitive!"

"Do I?" Northrup said with annoyance. "You're a free agent. Only I don't like the idea that you're wasting your energies elsewhere."

Donna chuckled. "Sweetheart! I got in before dawn. I'm still intact."

Northrup grumbled. "Sounds like a lively night."

"Strictly from nowhere, my pet."

"How long did it take to find out?" Northrup asked savagely.

"I had to be polite," Donna replied pleasantly. "Charming little man. Big black eyes, roly-poly figure, chubby cheeks, and clutching hands. He comes up to my middle. But frightfully rich. Imports East African coffee. Egyptian. He was after a date for months. Now he's had it."

"Where'd you go?"

"Flambeau Room. Lots of atmosphere, lousy food. Then this new musical and off to the Village for night life. Then this jazz joint with this trumpet blasting in my ear, after which a messy scene at my door with these frantic and sweaty hands. I'm not complaining, sweetheart, only showing you what we people in public relations have to contend with."

Northrup grunted, mollified. "Sounds like race prejudice, to me."

"Harry Northrup!" Donna said sharply. "That's a horrible thing to say. I haven't got an ounce of race prejudice in me. Not a speck."

"No?"

"Certainly not!"

"Everyone has."

"Not me!"

Northrup paused with meaning. "Would you fly in an Egyptian airplane?"

A thoughtful moment passed.

"You have a point," Donna conceded, but added spiritedly, "but I'd be glad to place their advertising for my usual fee. Doesn't that prove something? Now tell me,"—a sound of a match being struck floated over the wire—"can you help me get rid of the taste tonight? Dinner, movie, back here for a couple of drinks, and then a spot of cooperation between the sexes?"

Northrup waited. "Can't, darling. That's why I called."

Donna took it well enough. "Something come up?"

"More or less," Northrup said, hating the stupid position in which he found himself. "I'm catching a plane out of La Guardia at noon. I'm going up to Dannemora."

"But it's Saturday, darling. Can't it wait?"

"*It* can. *I* can't."

Donna was silent, and Northrup knew she was coming

to terms with disappointment. She said finally, "All right, darling. I understand."

"Angry?"

"Not angry. Just wondering why you bothered to call. You build me up and knock me down."

Northrup said slowly, "Just wanted to hear your voice. Helps me to visualize you in bed with your hair loose on the pillows."

"But duty comes first?"

"Something like that." Northrup stared grimly at the telephone. The sun would be streaming into Donna's bedroom, glinting through the chintz curtains, picking out the lively paintings on the wall, throwing into high relief her vivid coloring, and the room could be ringing with her hearty laughter, and the bed could be warm and inviting through the weekend. How could this thing be explained? "But not exactly duty," he added. "I'd be no fun in this mood. Sorry."

"No more than me," Donna said remotely. "I love you, darling, but time to brush my teeth. Enjoy your trip."

Northrup hung up, cursing the folly of his youthful choice of profession, and then walked the few blocks to the East Side Airlines Terminal on First Avenue and caught an early coach for La Guardia Airport.

Three hours of flying time over the mountainous terrain of upper New York State having elapsed, and a brisk reading of Kafka's *The Trial* behind him, Northrup arrived at Clinton Prison at Dannemora—Little Siberia of New York State. He liked *The Trial*—a prisoner accused, given no inkling of the charges, no clue to the witnesses, no benefit of counsel, merely exposure to the inquisitorial powers of the police state.

It tickled his sense of devotion to the time-honored procedures hammered out over a thousand years of development of Anglo-Saxon jurisprudence of which he was a representative.

The 20-foot wall loomed high above him. Warden Lee Brian welcomed Northrup with a grim smile. "Did that tape do you any good?"

"Some. I'm not sure yet. I've got to talk to Scarpa myself first. I'm not too sure where any of this is leading—if it's leading any place."

The prison man nodded intelligently, asking no questions,

observing the decorum of men who trade on good faith and secret dealings with each other.

"I listened myself," Brian said. "I'd say Malfino's trying to con Scarpa into something."

"That'll be the day."

Brian nodded. "I don't want to know details, Harry. But can you give me the nature of the operation?"

Northrup shrugged. "I don't know. It may be nothing. It might lead to international complications. Who can tell? Is Scarpa due to walk out?"

"Maybe next month."

"How come? He's not up for parole?"

"He volunteered for a medical experiment." Brian described the cancer implant. "It's worth a full commutation of sentence. At least, to allow parole. I'm positive."

Northrup frowned. "Is this known outside? Say, to Baldo's old friends?"

"Meaning Malfino?"

"Meaning Malfino."

Brian shrugged. "It was never announced. It's just between me, the Parole Commission, and the governor's secretary. But you know how it is, Harry."

"I know how it is."

Some moments passed. "How do you feel about letting Scarpa out?" Northrup asked.

Brian turned and stared at the sky. "I'm in favor of letting anybody out," he said. "I think Scarpa would be safe."

"Why? Because he's old?"

Brian shook his head. "No," he said briefly. "I think he's had enough. He wants out. Home. He's a man with strong feelings and good intelligence. He's got a grandchild he's never seen and that means a lot to him. He hasn't even seen his daughter since she was a kid."

"Yes, I know," Northrup mused.

"Do you?" Brian swung around speculatively, studying the lawyer's rugged, battered face. "You send 'em up, Northrup. I've got to live with 'em. I'm part of a penal institution, too—and I sit on a balance of forces all the time. Scarpa's got a sense of himself—"

"What kind of sense?"

"Humiliation," Brian said quietly. "He's been caged most of his life. That's not for a man. He's afraid of one thing

—being put back into the cage. Once more, and he's a four-
time loser, and he'll never see the outside—"

"Yes!" A recurrent theme, Northrup thought, the four-
time loser, the hopeless man in the hole, Château d'If, Ed-
mond Dantes, the world is mine! Never to see the outside!
He shivered, despite the heat.

Brian was continuing. "—he would die in a prison cell.
I don't think he would take the risk. Not on the balance.
In any case, the man earned this way out."

"Earned how?"

Brian reached for a buzzer and gave instructions to the
trusty who appeared before he answered the question.
"Would you let 'em plant cancer in your body, Northrup?
For anything?"

Northrup shivered. "No."

"He took his chance with cancer," Brian said grimly. "I
don't think a man who wants out that much will throw it
away. That trusty will show you the way."

Northrup waited, alone in a green-painted room, thinking
about a warship lying far to the south in the Hudson River
and a corpse stiffening behind a privet hedge. The door
opened and a guard entered, accompanied by an old man.

Northrup was not prepared for what the years had done.
The twenty-year old photograph was sharp in his mind. Now,
with interest, he compared it with what he saw. The face
was tanned and ruddy but the fire had gone out of the eyes.
They were mild, sad eyes now. The eyebrows were still
thick, but now white. A fringe of white hair lay across the
domed scalp. A diet of starches had coarsened and thickened the strong face, and teeth were missing, robbing the
lips of their force and the chin of its jutting boldness. It
was still a strong, bold face, reminiscent of fury, but seventeen years of prison had weathered its granite. A finger
trembled as the old man stood at attention.

Northrup glanced at the guard. "You can wait outside.
I'll tell you when I'm done."

"Right, Mr. Northrup."

They were alone in a bare room.

"Can I call you Baldo?" Northrup asked.

Scarpa shrugged. "Call me what you like. I'm just a
con." His voice was hoarse and apprehensive.

"Sit down." Northrup felt a tinge of curiosity in the presence of a legend of the underworld. In his own Hell's Kitchen boyhood, the name of Baldo Scarpa had been big.

Scarpa was waiting patiently.

Northrup said, "Baldo, my name is Harry Northrup—"

Scarpa nodded. "I know. New York County. You got a reputation, Mr. Northrup."

Northrup paused. "I hope it's a good reputation."

"Oh, sure. You're supposed to be fair."

"Ah." Northrup waited uncertainly. "I'm not here to make trouble, so relax. I'm just here for a chat. There's some talk you might be let out soon, eh?"

The strong face was without expression. "Maybe," Scarpa said. "It's up to the governor, I hear."

Northrup nodded and let a measure of time pass. In all these interviews, subtleties of mood, play and counterplay, nuance and suggestion, were dependent on the ebb and flow of time. Scarpa was waiting patiently, advancing no thoughts of his own.

Northrup said, "I was told about those cancer experiments. Where did they make the implant?"

"On the belly," Scarpa said. "It sloughed off. Didn't even leave a scar."

"Good, good," Northrup said. "But suppose it took?"

"I'd be dead," Scarpa shrugged, and a ghost of a smile crossed his face. "Mr. Northrup, what do you want with me?"

"Just here to chat," Northrup said. "What do you figure to do on the outside, Baldo?"

"The outside?" Scarpa gazed at a patch of blue sky at the window. "Who knows? I'll look around, talk to old friends, find a job. I figure to live with my daughter and her husband. He's a nice boy, and I'll try to live nicely. It's all I want out of life now—to live nicely, Mr. Northrup. Nicely, and quiet."

Northrup smiled grimly. "Is that possible, Baldo? Your name was big in the city. Don't tell me you'll be able to sit by the kitchen stove like an old bum? The mob won't let you live alone."

"The mob?" Scarpa's smile was disconcertingly ironical. "What mob? These are new people, Mr. Northrup; they won't remember Baldo Scarpa."

Northrup nodded appreciatively. "Maybe so, maybe not,

Baldo. Suppose some proposition comes your way? Some feeler where you could make a score?"

"That's a pipe dream!" But Northrup noticed the change of color, the sudden pallor. "It just couldn't be, they should want me. Baldo Scarpa is through! Baldo Scarpa is an old tired horse. All he wants is to die in a bed, with some woman to say the prayers, and maybe his little family to the funeral." The old man rose, clenching and unclenching his hands. "Mr. Northrup, I would be insane to listen to any proposition. I would be a four-time loser. I would die in this hole—"

Northrup interrupted, "You had a visitor, Baldo! I was just told about it. Malfino!"

"Malfino?" Scarpa halted, disconcerted. "So what? He's an old friend of the family."

"What did he want?"

"Naturally, I wrote my daughter I had hopes to get out of this hole after this cancer business. Malfino came up to tell me he would help me find some job." The little finger was trembling. "What's so wrong? It's a condition of parole— I got to have a job, a place to live, a decent home."

"How could Malfino help?"

"Through the church where he's got a job." Scarpa wet his lips. "What should I do, Mr. Northrup? Meet some character from the old days? Who else would help an old con but the family? Mr. Northrup, what do you *want*?"

"Nothing." Northrup arose and picked up his hat. "Baldo, I hope you appreciate that my visit here was an unusual thing —a sign of respect. I don't come running to every cheap hood in the state, but in your case I would go a long way to have an understanding."

Scarpa's voice rose nervously. "Understanding about *what*, Mr. Northrup? You been doing a lot of hinting, a lot of beating around the bush—"

"Just an understanding," Northrup said evenly. "It's just possible, when you get out, people will want to use you—"

"I will not be used!"

Northrup ignored the interruption. "Just remember, you might want to call me sometime for your own sake. You might want to get on the side of the law. You help me, Baldo, and I'll help you."

"Hey, what's this?" Scarpa cried. "What help? How help? I got nothing to help. I only want to live my life. I want to keep away from the law." He was becoming agitated. "You are trying to trap me, Mr. Northrup. You are trying to push me into something. You are spinning a web around me. But I have nothing for you. Why have you come here? Why must you do this to me?"

The interview suddenly had lost its point. Northrup said simply, "Just remember, when you get into the outside world and start to have some rough going, that there's one man you can trust, one man you can come to, and his name is Harry Northrup. That's all I want to tell you, Baldo."

He called the guard. Scarpa was returned to confinement. Northrup felt tense and jumpy. The vivid revelation of what time had done to Baldo Scarpa saddened and troubled him. He wondered how much of what he had been trying to tell Scarpa had really gotten across. The name of Carl Malfino had been mentioned between them—and that was all. The vaguest hint of a nebulous web that ultimately might lead to the solution of—what?

Northrup flew back to New York that night aboard a nearly empty DC-3. A cloudburst above Albany buffeted the ship mercilessly, and Northrup thought he was going to be air sick for the first time in his life. But he outlasted the storm. Shortly before eleven, they landed at La Guardia Airport. Northrup marched tiredly through the hundreds of yards of passageway that led from the field to the coach stand, and he got home a little after midnight.

He was fatigued but not sleepy. He kicked off his shoes, mixed himself a daiquiri, and settled down in his big overstuffed chair.

The weathered old face of Baldo Scarpa haunted him. He was not quite convinced.

What would the old man do when released? The pressures would be enormous. The taste of power had once been sweet—power, wealth, deference, influence. Was it really forgotten?

Good talk, but that was in the shadow of the prison walls. How would it look on the outside—in the shadow of vast buildings and hoards of wealth waiting for bold and determined men.

Was Scarpa the hulk he seemed to be? Or was that play-acting, the outward show of a cunning and ruthless man who had schemed and dreamt for seventeen years for the moment of release? Or did it well up from the depths of the soul? "But I have that within which passeth show; These but the trappings and the suits of woe!" Easily said, but an actor could say the lines. It took a man to mean them.

Was Scarpa a man?

What kind of a man?

How much did the commutation mean? Freedom, the outside, the waiting family? Ifs, ands, buts, and whereases whirled around in Northrup's mind, and with dismay he realized that the case had caught him. It obsessed him. It was the only way he knew how to work: enmeshed in the job. The job that would not let him sleep.

A second drink, and a third, and a grim fourth, and more, and sometime later his head hit the pillow and he was out like a light.

Northrup slept a full nine hours. He was a little surprised, when he awakened, that he had needed that much rest. But when he studied his face in the shaving mirror, he realized that he still looked tired. There were pouches forming under his incisive brown eyes. The skin of his cheeks was losing tone. He had skipped his vacation last summer when an Asian flu epidemic decimated his fellow prosecutors, and he was starting to feel the cumulative effect of steady work with only rare one- or two-day breaks.

He spashed water in his face and ran a comb through his tangle of thick black hair. With a bachelor's unconscious vanity, he searched for streaks of gray. Still none. His father's hair had been thick and black and curly till the day he died, and Northrup hoped for the same. It was one of his few manifestations of petty pride.

Northrup had thought, yesterday, that he might drive out to Brooklyn and try to find Carl Malfino at the church where he worked. But now Northrup decided against it. It was Sunday, and the church would be full of worshippers. It wasn't a good time to go. And he resolved to allow himself the luxury of a day off.

He went out for breakfast. It was past eleven-thirty when he returned. He phoned Donna.

"Oh. I didn't think you'd be back this early." She sounded surprised. "It's delightful to be recalled to mind so soon."

"I flew back last night," he said. "Listen, what are you doing today? Don't hold Saturday against me."

"Reading the Sunday *Times,* mostly. Why?"

"I feel restless. I want to get out of the city. How do you react to the idea of a picnic?"

"I react positively, doctor. I thing it's the best idea I've heard all morning."

"Suppose I pick you up at half past twelve. Will that give you enough time to assemble everything?"

She hesitated. "Let's see. I've got hamburgers in the freezer. Pickles, cole slaw, baked beans, knives, forks, napkins —mm. I won't have to do any shopping. Except for beer. I'm all out."

"I'll pick some up at a delicatessen on the way over," Northrup said. "There's charcoal in the car, and the grill's still clean from last summer."

"Should I bother bringing a bathing suit?"

Northrup glanced out the window at the elm tree that was his weather indicator. "Looks pretty windy out there I'd say it's still to early in the season for swimming. Of course, if you want to be decorative—"

"Never mind," Donna said. "Ring my bell at half past twelve. I'll be ready."

Putting down the phone, Northrup threw on an old suede jacket and a battered pair of shoes that he had had at least five years, and went out. He walked up to the kosher delicatessen on Third Avenue, which was open on Sundays, and bought half a dozen bottles of Heineken's. "Throw in a bottle opener," he told the proprietor. He still grinned over the time when—despite his fine mind for detail—he had forgotten a bottle opener on a picnic and they had had to pry the caps up against the bumper of the car.

He double-parked in front of Donna's building and rang the bell. She was down almost immediately, carrying two wicker baskets full of provisions. Northrup took them from her and stowed them in the back seat of the Buick.

"How's Mr. D.A. this morning?" she asked, smiling.

"Surviving. How's Miss Madison Avenue?"

"Passable. I'm so glad you called, Harry. I was just wondering what the devil I was going to do today."

"So was I. Which is why I called." He grinned at her

and they got into the car. Donna was a tall girl, a shade over five feet six in stockinged feet, which made her just about as tall as Northrup when she wore high heels. Right now, though, her outfit was far from the usually dressy one he associated her with. She wore tight turquoise pedalpushers that accented the sleek line of her long legs and her hips, and a cotton pullover against which her full breasts thrust with agreeable steepness.

He started the car and headed east, toward the Franklin D. Roosevelt Drive. Smiling faintly, he wondered how the many men he had sent to prison would react if they knew that Harry Northrup was on a Sunday cookout in the country.

Donna said, "Did you accomplish much yesterday?"

"I'm not sure. I did what I could."

"This is some new case, isn't it?"

"Yes."

"Carlos Pereira?"

"What made you think of it?"

Donna smiled thinly as Northup cut around a slow-moving old sedan filled with children and anxious parents and sped toward the Willis Avenue Bridge. "I wonder, Harry, if you really grasp the larger world in which we public relations people function? When Trujillo was the bad boy of the Caribbean, he hired—"

"A lawyer!"

"A lawyer, yes! But one working in the larger calling of the public relations expert. Wasn't it Aristotle who wrote in *Ethics*— Or was it the *Politics*—that the highest profession in the hierarchy was the art of public relations?" Donna squinted against the bright sun.

"Never heard of that," Northrup grinned.

"Must be one of his lost writings," Donna decided. "If Aristotle didn't say it, he would have, if he'd been here. In any case, nations rise and fall, depending on the image projected against history. In a sense, Moses was the greatest P.R. man of 'em all—"

"What's that got to do with Pereira?"

"Oh, Pereira!" Donna had been rattling on. She studied her hands. "I'm not at liberty to divulge my sources, Harry, but this murder has been very upsetting to our hotel interests. We were just closing a deal with the Hilton people for a six-hundred-room structure. But now something's gone wrong."

"Wrong how?"

Donna was entirely serious. "Harry, the most sensitive people in any country, and the sharpest, are the hotel and tourist people. They deal in atmospherics, nuances, moods. One day, a country is a happy country where the peso is low and the tourist can get the runs for very little. Everybody makes money. The next, the country is sour, nobody cares for her at any price. Suddenly, since the Pereira murder, I can't sell my clients."

"I'm sorry."

"You're not, but I am. Little stories I usually can plant without trouble—the *Times*, the *Saturday Review*—are coming back. Travel agents are shunning us. They're fawning on the U.S.S.R., and Cairo and Damascus flourish like the green bay tree. But our country is anathema. Rumors are circulating that Pereira was assassinated by the old general."

"El Presidente?"

"Himself," Donna agreed. "It seems that Pereira was trying to set up a Buick assembly plant below the equator, and that El Presidente was neglecting the necessary legislation and tax benefits to make it possible—"

Northrup stared suspiciously. "You're kidding?"

"Not entirely," Donna said equably. "Something went wrong with Pereira's relationship with his government. What it might be, I can't tell you. I can only tell you that the room goes silent at the Consulate when his name is mentioned. You see, I have been working for you, my darling."

"What's their national anthem? The Coca Leaf Forever?"

"Something like that," Donna said elliptically. "Now tell me who you went to see in the Big House?"

"An old guy. I think he's headed for trouble."

"Connected with Pereira's murder?"

"No, no! But he might get involved. It would be a lead." Northrup paused to stare at his rear-view mirror. "I wouldn't want to see him involved."

Donna said with surprise, "Since when were you sentimental about jailbirds? This is Northrup?"

Northrup refused to respond to teasing. "You think I like to send a man up?" he asked wonderingly. "This isn't easy work. This old man has spent the best part of his life in prison. He wants to get out to live quietly with his daughter and grandson for the time left to him. I want to believe he means it."

"But?"

"But he may not get that chance," Northup said grimly.

"Who could stop him?"

"Me." Northrup lifted his hand and crooked a finger. "All it takes is this, and he stays in for life." He returned his hand to the wheel.

"Oh, I see!" Donna found it necessary to comb her hair and fix a face that needed no fixing. "Must you use him?"

"Maybe. I don't like it."

"Is someone twisting your arm?" Northrup flushed, and Donna went on. "You don't even need the job. I seem to remember some lush offers to practice law on the outside?"

"I'm good at it. Because it's got to be done."

"Because you enjoy it?"

"No!" A pause. "Well, maybe! But that's why I'm good at it. But not this part. Not deciding who lives, who dies, who stays in, who goes out! I'm a prosecutor," Northrup added savagely. "I'm no damn judge. Never took a really judgmental position in my life. I wouldn't feel adequate for that job. I can't understand men who can." He suddenly put his foot to the brake.

"Hey, what?"

The road had turned to the west and Northrup indicated, far to the south, the gray vessel, bristling with guns, dipping in the heavy tidal swell of the lower reaches of the river. Then his eyes caught a pennant flying and lettering showing its national origin. Or so it seemed. All of this was too distant to be clearly visible.

"The answer might be on that ship," he muttered.

"Oh, how?"

"I don't know! But something!" Northrup drove on, glancing aside speculatively. "Darling?"

"Yes, dear?"

"Could you get me on?"

"On the *Balthazar*?" Donna said doubtfully. "I thought we'd given up that thought?"

"Yes."

"Just go on."

"I'd have to explain myself. I mean, without their knowing who's asking."

Donna stared at Northrup. His dark features were flushed.

In their years together, he had not once put her so close to his workaday world.

"Is it important?" she asked.

"Yes." Northrup was silent. "I'm not sure where all this is leading. I've got a murder of a man who spent time on that ship. He's been visited by three men who came here on that ship. Now, a local gunman is contacted, and he's up there at Dannemora talking to an old man. I can't see any pattern, but there's a force radiating from that vessel. I feel it. I sense it. It doesn't let me alone."

Donna was silent. "I'll think about it," she promised. "I'd be glad to help, but I don't see how."

Less than an hour later, Northrup brought the car to a halt in the state park not far from Peekskill. It had a shallow lake, and a rambling path that led through unspoiled woods. They selected a table on the edge of the lake.

Hours later, with a cold wind blowing from the north, they drove back to the city, sated with laziness and the peace of the countryside in spring. It was dark on 56th Street when they reached Donna's apartment.

"Would you like to come up?" she asked. "I'll crack open a bottle."

"What about dinner?" he asked.

"Later."

The apartment was neat and beguiling—modern prints, hi-fi, Swedish furiture, and an inviting bed covered by a white candlewick spread. Donna found a bottle of rum.

"Daiquiris?"

"God willing," Northrup said. "Because I am."

They had a drink apiece, and then, smiling, amused at each other, they put their drinks aside and strolled into the bedroom where a timeless rite was performed.

Monday morning, Northrup was at his desk early to pick up threads of a weekend investigation on lines earlier laid down. First a report on the *Balthazar*. No news there. Sailors, still at liberty, had not returned from weekend furlough, nor had anyone else come aboard or left. It lay at anchor, isolated, alone, menacing.

The Morales delegation, as reported by Duyckman and Rodriquez, had been busy at unexceptional tasks. They had held a party for the Spanish-language press. They had visited well-dressed men of Latin appearance, some with beards, but no contacts of suspicious nature with underworld characters. Certainly not with Malfino. Northrup lit his twelfth cigarette for the morning and reached for the telephone.

"Mr. Vyborg?"

The Scandinavian responded with caution. "This is he! I am quite busy."

"About Pereira?"

"We have more important assassinations to consider," the United Nations official responded tartly. "Our newly emerged brothers in a certain continent are engaging in that sport of kings. If you'll excuse me?"

"One minute!"

"Yes, Mr. Northrup?"

"Has his delegation considered replacing him on that committee?"

"To negotiate the treaty for setting quotas?"

"Of narcotics."

"Ah, yes! Yes, I believe so."

"Who's going to replace him?"

A pause.

'Señor Francisco Morales," Vyborg said. Northrup realized that the neighing sound he heard could not be equine but respresented a Scandinavian response to a situation of humor. "It is incredible," Vyborg went on, biting his dentals, "but an *entente cordiale* is brewing between that delegation and the delegation from the Pearl of the Antilles. Officially, the dictatorships loathe each other, but on some issues they make common cause. We can expect charges, I think, that the heavy purchases by your country of opium stocks are subjecting the producing countries of the crop—Iran, Turkey, Burma, India, China—to economic enslavement. Countries where opiates are the religion of the people. *Tak tak!*" he chuckled, signing off in Swedish.

Later that morning, Northrup found himself on the eighth floor of the Criminal Courts Building, facing the level gaze of the District Attorney of New York County. Leonard Farrell, a compact, athletic man of fifty, was vexed to be diverted from a more sensational homicide—an international financier murdered in a Sutton Place penthouse.

"You're taking a hell of a time over Pereira," Farrell growled, passing over a cigar.

"Complaints?"

"Naturally." Farrell blew a plume of blue smoke. "You've been squatting on this homicide. Meanwhile, El Presidente is pestering Washington for reports, and action. If you don't show results, some boys in cloaks will be here with daggers for you and me. Maybe the glory boys from the F.B.I. What chance has our press representative got against theirs? In the race for headlines, Harry," Farrell said instructively, "if conscience stands between this office and national publicity, grab the publicity."

"Naturally," said Northrup.

The lazy banter went on until the cigar was finished. Yet it was not altogether banter. The experienced prosecutors, holding public office of extreme vulnerability, were keenly aware of the need to maintain public confidence. Northrup brought his chief up to date on the thin hopes which lay in the surveillance of Carl Malfino and Baldo Scarpa.

Farrell swung about with interest. "Scarpa? You think the old man's involved?"

Northrup shrugged. "I don't know," he said candidly. "It's just that the air is suddenly polluted. I don't like this much coincidence." Briefly, he outlined the threads that led from the site of murder at Riverside Park to the great prison at Dannemora. "It could be something. Or nothing. I've got nothing more to go on. And if this delegation from chinchilla country is pulling something fast, I can't tip my mitt. Too much Indian blood runs under those copper skins to try pressure."

"Scarpo, sure!" A smile of fond reminiscence lit Farrell's face. He was old enough to recall the heroic figures of the Prohibition era. "What connection could there be? South America's a long way off."

"Is it?"

"I think so."

"Maybe it is."

A pause.

"The Scarpa file wouldn't support that view," Northrup said finally. "Testimony in this 1943 file. Scarpa spent some winters in South America in the late Thirties. He was accused of running Venezuelan rum into Louisiana, but the charge was dropped. Izzy and Moe were heartbroken. And in 1940, Bolivian tax authorities picked him up for smuggling American autos into their country without paying duty. Stolen autos, let me add. Scarpa had a relative in the consulate quash the charge, and he left for Colombia."

"A relative?"

"A relative of his lawyer's," Northrup grinned. "In any case, Scarpa left a trail in South America."

"It's a big continent," Farrell grunted after a hard stare.

"Scarpa was a big man!" Northrup retorted. "They're making television programs out of his life. Frankly, I think it's a shame the way these television people pick on these poor, helpless cons, making fat livings out of their misery, etcetera. Do the families ever get compensated? They do not—"

Farrell cut into the flow, annoyed. "All right, so Baldo Scarpa cut a swath thirty years ago south of the border. What about Malfino? The son of a bitch was raised in our own back yard. Yankee, all the way through."

Northrup grinned. "Oh, sure!" he agreed. "Home grown, but out of Argentine stock," he added, after some irritating byplay with a cigar stub. "His mother was born in Buenos Aires. Malfino's papa met her when he was in the export trade, before he got all this respectability in sand and gravel, and that branch of the family is spread throughout the continent. Somebody got in touch with somebody."

"Why?" Farrell growled.

"I'm trying to find out," Northrup replied, unruffled. "Morales plus Malfino equals MC squared."

"You hope?"

"I hope," Northrup agreed. "In any case, this hope is a thread which might lead us out of darkness. For some reason, like dominoes falling, one thing leads to another. I've got to watch them fall."

Farrell arose, and the conference was at an end. The talk had been light, but the purpose deadly.

"By the way," Farrell concluded, closing the door on his luxurious suite, "I've made an appointment for you with a guy named Harley. Try to shine those shoes. I'd like to have you make a good impression on the State Department. And where do you get those suits? Ackerman's?"

"Pay me more," Northrup retorted, "and I'll try De Pinna.

What's this about the State Department? They haven't been doing so good! If it's political advice, I can tell 'em to read Walter Lippman. I do."

The club on Park Avenue was a ponderous castle, squat and heavy among all the airy skyscrapers of glass that lined the avenue. Northrup was staring uneasily at steel engravings and oil paintings of a past century when a smooth, well-oiled voice disturbed his thoughts.

"Mr. Northrup?"

Northrup turned about. "Right."

"Baxter Harley. Glad to meet you. Heard so many fine things about you from the Attorney General. He used to work in your office?"

"Dick Hunt? Oh, sure! How's he doing?"

Harley smiled carefully. "Well, he *is* a lawyer!" he said in the tones of a minister about to baptize a first baby— enigmatic but hearty. "Lunch?"

Baxter Harley was slick, Northrup decided. Forty-five, tall and straight-backed, with square shoulders and iron-gray hair —a sort of dramatic handsomeness that made Northrup uncomfortable. Harley's elegant tweeds, which clung to his athletic frame, made the prosecutor suddenly conscious of his own frayed cuffs and heavily padded shoulders, a style which had grown several years out of date. They walked through the hush of reading rooms complete with red leather armchairs, subdued lighting and copies of the *Wall Street Journal*.

"Cocktail?"

"Very dry," Northrup said.

Cocktails came and went while Baxter Harley politely made conversation in accents manufactured on the Charles River in Massachusetts. Northrup grunted, occasionally rubbing a broken nose, conscious that diction was not a strong point at Fordham University. He was equally conscious of vague dislike. He was bored with a long defense of the position taken by the State Department on the Middle East.

"Harley—" he broke in.

The State Department man was on his fifth cocktail. "Baxter," he suggested. "Call me Baxter."

"Baxter," Northrup amended. "Tell me something?"

"Sure."

"Why are you people always out of step?"

Harley frowned. "Out of step with what?"

"With the interests of the country."

"Are we?"

"I think so." Northrup was quite serious. "In every country in the world we've got politicians scolding, brow-beating, blackmailing us with one threat. If we don't pay up, they threaten to join Russia. Why don't we let 'em?"

"You're not serious?" Harley asked with concern.

"Sure I am," Northrup said with warmth. "Our friends are getting fed up. It doesn't pay to be a friend of this country. What does it get? A kick in the teeth. Take Pakistan—"

"Yes?"

"They're hooked up to us with treaty obligations. But India gets the fat deal that pays off. Neutral India. Why aren't we neutral if it's such a wonderful policy?" Northrup polished off his Gibson and called for a seventh. "Take that last trouble with China. Why didn't we tell that guy in diapers we would be neutral in any fracas with Red China?"

Harley smiled painfully. "We can't afford that. They wouldn't believe us."

"Would they believe you if students from City College paraded in front of the United Nations?"

Harley looked startled. "I think they would," he said thoughtfully, and made a note in a little red book. "Hindu, go home!" He tried out the phrase several times. "Good thinking."

"Or take this campaign against us from Cairo," Northrup went on warmly. "We save that guy's neck, he plays footsie with the Russians, they give him guns and planes and submarines, and we beg him to take our money. Harley, who makes these decisions?"

"We do," Harley said uncomfortably.

"Who's we?" Northrup raised his voice. "Why don't we ever get the name of the guy who makes the decision? Why must it always be the anonymous spokesman? And why? Why?" he went on, finding it difficult to speak against a tongue thickened with alcohol. "Why in every crisis are we told that the State Department isn't surprised? The Russians fire a Sputnik and the *Times* reports that the State Department isn't surprised. They take over Tibet, and the State Department isn't surprised. If they're never surprised, why can't we get the benefit of their foreknowledge for a change?"

"What good is it to be surprised?" Harley asked.

"None, I guess, but it's less irritating."

"For example," Harley went on with an edge of nastiness, "would you be surprised to know that we'd rather you kept your nose clean about the *Balthazar?*"

Northrup dropped his glass. *"Balthazar?"*

"Surprised?"

"Sure."

"Does it make you feel good?"

"No," Northrup admitted. "I figured you had something to tell me about Carlos Pereira and that trio of Morales boys. *Balthazar* was my information. What's on that ship?"

"Cocaine," Harley said, baring even white teeth with surprising good humor.

Northrup waited. "How much?"

"Lots. On the retail market—"

"I know. On the retail market, it's worth millions. It always is. Cocaine, hey?" Northrup frowned as hints and rumors suddenly fell into place. "Is it really a lot? Are you sure?"

"It's definite, all right. We've got a man in Valparaiso who transmits information occasionally. It seems that he's got a cousin on that ship who's got a special assignment. To keep guard on a certain room where the stuff is held."

"I see."

Northrup looked up into frosty gray eyes which suddenly seemed to deserve more respect than he had been giving. He said, "Held for whose benefit?"

"Juan Morales."

"The Commissioner of Internal Affairs? Brother to Francisco? Father to Pascual and Diego?"

"Exactly."

Northrup put aside an empty glass. "What's the ploy?"

"As you may know, the Commissioner of Internal Affairs grants licenses to coca leaf growers throughout the country. The country as a whole has an over-all quota established at regular intervals by an international treaty negotiated and administered by the United Nations. This gives him certain, ah, influence over the warehouses where the stuff is kept. It would not be too hard to imagine circumstances under which a given quantity would stick to his hands."

"Not hard at all," Northrup agreed.

Harley said, "It would be awkward if Morales managed to sell that stuff in this country."

"I imagine it would."

"Not for the usual reasons. Narcotics are bad. But that's your headache and the Treasury people's, not mine."

"What's your angle?"

Harley said, "As you know, we recognize the regime of the president, General Villaneuva, but we're not too happy with the old boy. Country's stagnating. Villanueva takes our money and builds palaces while his son spends it on Hollywood starlets. That sort of thing."

"Get rid of him."

Harley looked shocked. "Can't! That would be interference. The old boy's no tyrant. Just improvident. What we're doing is to keep an eye open for likely factions who might be worth our support when the time comes. In the power vacuum, there'll be a scramble and we hope that a friendly faction will come into control.

"Anyone in mind?" Northrup asked innocently.

Harley looked equally innocent. "One man doesn't make us too unhappy. He understands his country's needs and he promises to guide it toward reasonable democracy."

"We've had promises before," Northrup observed.

"Haven't we?" Harley agreed cheerfully. "Still, if we weren't raped regularly, I think we'd feel lonely and unloved. This man is now flawless, but he's on our side. Allegedly."

"And Juan Morales?"

Harley pursed his mouth. "The rumor is that Morales is growing a beard. He's had enough strength to force Villanueva to concede that post as Commissioner of Internal Affairs. It seemed innocuous at the time, because power rests with the army and the police, but if he can sell the stuff here, he can buy the arms for a quick change of government—long enough to install himself as the maximum *Jefe* of his country. That's the real danger of this stuff—its value for guns, automatic weapons, a big supply for a quick move. It would be Cuba all over again. We don't want Morales to move that stuff."

"But you want me to keep away from the *Balthazar*?"

"Exactly." Harley said with an edge, "We don't want another false move on our record. Boarding a warship of a friendly country would just do it. And what would you gain?"

"Nothing, I expect."

Northrup considered several disagreeable angles. "Where did Pereira fit into all this?"

"Oh, Pereira," Harley frowned, having completely forgotten

the origin of Northrup's investigation. "Friend of General Villaneuva, maybe. Maybe not. Or perhaps he was holding out for too much. In any case, his position at the U.N. was probably too uncomfortable. Does it matter?"

"I believe murder matters," Northrup said grimly.

Harley was suddenly bored. "Perhaps it does," he agreed carelessly. "But that's your problem, isn't it?"

Northrup waited. "Just one thing, Harley—"

"Oh, yes?"

"Who told you I was interested in the *Balthazar*?"

Harley removed his glasses, managing to look urbane and amused all at once. "Strictly between us, Northrup," he observed, "your friend, Miss Donna Reynolds, is registered with us as the representative of a foreign country. Occasionally we trade information." He snapped his fingers and called for two fine brandies—the best in stock. "She made a most determined effort on your behalf, informally, of course, to get clearance to arrange for your presence on that ship. So sorry nothing came of it." He was smiling as he finished off his drink.

Back in his office, Northrup stared at Carl Malfino's file. The role of the *Balthazar* was clear—a deadly white powder, the antidote for misery in its country of origin, the source of misery and criminality in its country of destination. But still he was no closer to the murder of Carlos Pereira. Where would Malfino's file lead?

Joe Scott had handled that trial six years earlier. Malfino and another man had held up a lithography firm on payroll day. The company treasurer had been cornered in an elevator, struck unconscious, and relieved of $12,000. Police had found Malfino at home in possession of the money. He had drawn five to ten years at Clinton Prison at Dannemora on a reduced plea, and he had been let out on parole after four years and some months.

Looking at a prison photograph, Northrup saw a man with black eyes, a strong curved nose, full lips and fat cheeks. The chin was pointed. There was unsmiling menace in the expression, the sheathed deadliness of a leopard's paw. Northrup reached for the telephone and asked for Joe Scott.

"Yup?"

"Joe, you remember Carl Malfino?"

"Oh, sure. Mean bastard. Why?"

"Parole Board findings here say he's been a model prisoner. Religious awakening. Parole recommended. Would you believe those findings?"

Scott sounded abstracted and muffled. "Who knows? St. Paul was a scourge until he had a vision. Why not Carl Malfino? I hear he's got a job in some church in Brooklyn. Has he done anything?"

"I'm not sure." Northrup asked, "What would make him visit Baldo Scarpa?"

"Why not? Friend of the family."

"You say that in a funny way."

"Sure. The friend was Baldo's daughter."

"Helen?"

"Sure. Helen was a beautiful kid. She and Malfino were trailing around together. Real big torch she was carrying for him. Of course she got married when he went up."

"Married who?"

"Some Irish guy." Scott was beginning to show impatience. "Look, Harry, unless you've got something on your mind, form your own opinion about Malfino. I'm not his father. I just sent him up for a stretch. That doesn't make me a marriage counselor—"

"Don't hang up, Joe."

"What else? Harry, I'm busy! I've got an abortion case I'm preparing—"

"Joe!"

"Yes?"

"What did you mean, 'Of course Helen got married when Malfino got sent up'?"

"Nice Italian girl—what else would she do? Go in for politics?" Scott's irritation was rising. "What are you driving at, Harry? It was a routine robbery one. With a gun. I gave Carl Malfino a break when I let him plead guilty to robbery in the third degree, and he drew an easy sentence. Are you trying to review my case?"

"No, Joe, of course not." Northrup hesitated, and came to the gnawing question. "Just this. Here we have Baldo Scarpa's daughter rolling in the hay with Malfino, a college man from Notre Dame, and things happen. You never yet let a gun robbery get reduced to robbery in the third. How come Malfino got that break?"

A long silence passed.

"Harry, I handle my file the way I see fit," Scott said quietly. "You handle yours, or I'll take it up with the boss—"

"Just a minute."

"What now?"

"According to the file, Malfino had a mask on during the stickup. How did the police know enough to pull a raid on him the next morning? Who tipped them off?"

Another silence. "The police had a confidential informant," Scott said with anger. "They didn't tell me, and I didn't ask. As for Baldo Scarpa, he's just a memory. The family connection had nothing to do with my decision."

The telephone went dead.

Northrup turned about thoughtfully and lit a pipe. One more aspect of a complex mess to be studied. In time. Meanwhile other things came first.

7

The Church of the Holy Name was a pile of masonry on Flatbush Avenue in Brooklyn's busiest section. The church was empty but for a few worshippers in a side chapel. In the rear, a gray-haired priest came out of one of the confessionals.

"Father?"

The priest turned and a look of expectation died at the appearance of a stranger. "Can I help you?"

Northrup explained his mission. "I'd like to talk about one of the men who works here. Carl Malfino."

"Is he in trouble?" the priest asked quickly.

"Not that I know of," Northrup replied.

The priest hesitated. "Come this way." He led the way to a door that looked upon a rear garden. "That's Carl now," Father Giardino said quietly. Malfino looked up from trimming the hedges and smiled, and waved, and the priest waved back. It was as though some instinct told him that he was under discussion.

"Don't forget the forsythia, Carl," the priest said indulgently.

"Next on my list," Malfino replied with a show of strong white teeth. His lips, Northrup noticed, were deep red against the dark olive skin. It struck him suddenly that Malfino was remarkably handsome in a sensual, compelling style. With his shirtsleeves rolled back, his forearms were powerful with the easy play of serpentine muscles. In that instant, the black eyes had seemed to weigh him in the balance. Northrup shivered.

"This way," the priest said.

The office was small and austere with a plain desk on which sat a ledger book and a copy of the Bible. Father Giardino waited quietly, staring at Northrup with faint hostility. "I must tell you," he said evenly, "that I do not approve of these constant visits from the authorities. All the value of my work with Carl is put in jeopardy. How can I help you?"

Northrup lit a cigarette. "How long has he worked here, Father?"

"He has been with us since he left prison. It was a condition of parole that he have a job. We are happy with him."

"What does he do?"

"He takes care of the garden. He cleans the church building. He runs errands. Little jobs."

"Does he take part in the observances?"

"Occasionally we let him carry a candle. That's as far as we can go at the moment."

"At the moment? Does that imply that eventually he'll be given more responsibilities?"

Farther Giardino searched Northrup's hard, skeptical face. "I have great hopes for Carl," he said quietly. "I think this place is good for him. I see a great change in his attitudes."

"From what he has told you?"

Father Giardino smiled with reserve. "We judge a tree by its fruit. I think Carl has come a long way. But since you are not his parole officer, Mr. Northrup, can you tell me exactly what you want?"

Northrup mentioned a group of names. "Do you know any of those men?"

"I know their families from the neighborhood. They are parishioners. Why?"

"Have any of them come to talk to Malfino?"

The priest shrugged. "I haven't noticed. You understand, I try not to spy on Carl. I want him to feel that he has my confidence. Is there any special reason you can give me for this visit?"

"Not yet," Northrup said, rising. "Oh, one more question. I hope you won't mind?"

The priest rose. "What is your question?"

Northrup said, "Has Malfino ever confided the circumstances under which he was arrested and sent to prison? I am not asking of course about privileged matters."

The priest thought. "No," he said finally. "Not even in the confession."

"Then how good was his last confession?"

Father Giardino opened the door. "I am sure his prior confessions were full, and good, and I have no doubts that Carl is making every effort to redeem himself. Goodbye, Mr. Northrup."

"Goodbye, Father."

Vaguely discomfitted, Northrup left. As he passed, he paused to study the powerful man clipping the hedges. Privet hedges. Sweet smelling after their watering, reminiscent of the hedges in Riverside Park where the clay of Carlos Pereira had been found. Malfino did not look up. He clipped with precision. A devout man? A sinner turned saint? Or a cunning man using a novel place to keep his activities in concealment. Northrup returned to his car and drove back to Manhattan. It would be only a matter of weeks before Baldo Scarpa left prison.

Parole Officer Maestroangeli appeared at Northrup's office looking worried and unhappy.

"It's about Malfino, Mr. Northrup."

Northrup finished signing a recommendation for a D.O.R. —that an old indictment for burglary be dismissed for lack of prosecution. "What about him?"

Maestroangeli said, "He tried to put in the fix. He tried to pay off one of my men."

"Not unusual," Northrup said mildly. "Did your man take it?"

The parole officer opened an envelope, initiated by himself and his superior, and spread a sheaf of bills on the desk. Ten twenty-dollar bills. Two hundred crackers. A good hunk of change for anyone.

A muscle began to throb in Northrup's cheek. "What's this all about?" he said sharply. "Didn't we agree to let Malfino out on a string?"

"Pure accident, Mr. Northrup," Maestroangeli said de-

fensively. "Ed Tompkins was off duty Saturday night, and
he was out on the town with his girl friend. They wound
up at a spot in the East Side, downtown, one of these jazz
dumps, sitting with a couple of drinks, and who is sitting
three tables away but Malfino?"

"In a night club?" Northrup murmured. "That's gall."

"You know criminals," Maestroangeli observed.

"Oh, sure!"

"No sense."

"None at all," Northrup agreed.

Maestroangeli raised three fingers. "Three regulations he's
breaking all at once—no drinks, no running around without letting his parole officer know, no wrong-o associations.
Outside Brooklyn, sitting in a night club, stinking with
whisky, and this woman he's with! You know who she is?"

"Brigitte? Gina? Marilyn? Jane?"

"Nah! Helen Keleher." Northrup looked blank. "Helen
Scarpa Keleher," Maestroangeli added smugly.

Northrup looked up. "Baldo's daughter?"

"Right! To hear Ed Tompkins, she was dolled up fit
to knock you over. A neckline down to here"—a pudgy
finger lodged over his navel—"and perfume, and makeup
and everything. Ed has a couple in him, and he wants to
impress the girl friend. So he waltzes over and he says something like, 'You know you got no business here, Carl.'"
Maestroangeli mimicked a hoarse Brooklyn voice. "Then
Malfino claims this Helen is one he used to be serious
about, only it's her wedding anniversary and the husband's
too busy to take her out so he's standing in for the guy."

"Standing in how far?" Northrup asked.

Maestroangeli closed his eyes in an effort of recollection.
"He didn't say," he conceded. "So Ed wants to throw some
weight. He calls Malfino aside and tells him he's going to
pull him in for violation of parole."

The two men exchanged glances.

"I hate to say this," Northrup finally remarked. "But you've
got a first-class shlock working for you."

"I told you, Mr. Northrup, Ed Tompkins had a skinful."

Northrup made a discouraged gesture. "Go on!"

"Tompkins says Malfino was kind of smug," Maestroangeli went on with a touch of wonder. "Kind of a superior
smile. Maybe he was high. I'm not sure."

"What does that mean?"

Maestroangeli hesitated. "Well! The man can be weird at times. He can be tossed into the can like *that!*" The parole officer snapped his fingers. "But with those eyes, he's kind of measuring like he has the answers. Like he can move you around—"

Northrup studied a troubled face. "Go on," he said briefly.

Maestroangeli cleared his throat. "Well! He put his arm around Ed Tompkins and asks if they can go into a corner. Ed was just tanked enough to say, 'Why not? Why not? What'sa harm inna corner?' "

"Yeah, what?" Northrup agreed. "What happened in this corner?"

Maestroangeli screwed up his face in an effort at precision. "This, and that," he recalled, "and finally the man asks Ed if they can talk the matter over. Would Ed be reasonable, or must he go back and finish up his time? Ed had a problem."

"Problem?"

"This girl friend was sending him signals. And what the hell! We all look the other way some time. Besides, being married, what was he doing there himself? He said, sure, he would be reasonable, and gave a wink, and went back to his own table where he made the high sign. Malfino left, but this morning an envelope came with these bills." Maestroangeli spread out the sheaf of legal tender. Ed Tompkins wouldn't take a wrong dollar to save his life. But with his criminal mentality, I guess Malfino thought he bought himself a man."

Northrup considered the matter. "Malfino doesn't know about this?"

"Guess not. I don't think a man with that experience would try to put in the fix unless he had the idea that he had got the man lock, stock, and barrel. Look, this thing has gone a lot too far now. When a guy starts putting a shmear on one of my guys, I got to tell the State Board about it. This is serious! It's enough to send Malfino back to Dannemora for a nice long trip! This is real anti-social!"

Northrup was silent a moment. Then he said, "Let it ride, Dom."

"I can't, Mr. Northrup. I've overlooked all sorts of ir-regularities in Malfino's conduct these past couple weeks, on account of you asked me to. He's been seeing guys at that church, and that South American bird outside, and I've been letting it ride. But a fix is different. I got to file a report on it. It's a big offense, fixing the parole board. A man like that shouldn't be left loose."

"I want you to let it ride, Dom," Northrup said in a quiet voice. "You tell Tompkins that from now on he's to wink at anything Malfino does. He's to keep an eye on him, sure, and to report everything—but no arrest. Let Malfino think he's got Tompkins in his pocket."

"Would you mind telling me just what the hell kind of operation you're running?"

"We've gone over this," Northrup said patiently. "I don't want pressure."

Maestroangeli sighed. "I'm not happy."

"Neither am I, Dom. Believe me."

The parole officer drummed the desk. "Okay, okay! I went along on that first trip to Dannemora. But this is entirely a different horse. I can overlook a lot, but a thing like this?" He stared unhappily. "I like my work, Mr. Northrup. I'd hate to be out on the street."

"Let it ride, Dom. Let it ride."

Maestroangeli grumbled, but the decision was made. Malfino would remain out on a string. The Parole Board would play along.

Alone, Northrup turned toward the City Prison and cracked his kuckles thoughtfully. Malfino was surprisingly clumsy, he thought. Or something was up. Something important. Time, and the appearance of Baldo Scarpa would tell. One thing was sure. Despite Father Giardino, they were not dealing with a saint. A note on his desk told him that the *Balthazar* had gone off to Newport News, Virginia, on a visit of state and would soon be back.

PART TWO

8

It was the second week of May, now. The weather, which had been unseasonably cold a month earlier, now grew unseasonably hot as summer made a premature arrival. The temperature was in the eighties the day that Baldo Scarpa stepped through the gates of Clinton Prison and into the open air.

The old man blinked in the sunlight. He felt a qualm of fear as he took his first steps of freedom. Seventeen years!

"You look great, Baldo!" the guard said.

"Yeah?"

"You just look a million! Don't come back!"

"Thanks, Father!"

Baldo turned to thank the prison chaplain and put the prison firmly behind him. At the station, without escort, he waited for the train, thinking that the world had changed. In his first years at Clinton Prison, he had not kept up with events. The grapevine brought news of friends and associates, in and out of the prison system throughout the country, but for general events he had had no stomach. A prison break in Michigan had meant more than the Korean War. But in the last weeks of his stay, he had worked like fury in the prison library to lay his hands on newspapers and books of current interest.

Television. Jet planes. New names. Not Roosevelt or Churchill or Stalin or Hitler or Mussolini. A lot of new people. New names.

On the train, Baldo sat by himself, uncomfortable in his new civilian suit, uncomfortable in freedom. He was a tall, dignified man with a forbidding face, white-haired and venerable, but he felt unclean and alone. A group of chattering children on their way between stations on the local stops disconcerted him and he gazed out at pasture and timberland and the lovely countryside of America and put his thoughts ahead. The letter said Helen would meet him at the station, along with her husband, and the baby, and maybe Carl Malfino. Baldo shivered. Why Malfino? Maybe Helen and her husband—what was his name?

Baldo found himself sweating. He could not remember the name of his own son-in-law suddenly. Was he going crazy? Was the mind softening?

And then the name popped into mind. Jim! Jim Keleher! Sure, an Irish name, Jim Keleher. He kept repeating the name, afraid that he might forget—forget what? Oh, God! This happened in stir—a man's brains got scrambled, and then what was he good for? What was the outside? *You look great, Baldo! You just look a million. Don't come back!* Yeah, Jim Keleher, and Helen, and Tommy, and— *Malfino!*

Yeah, I look great! Great for what? For a cup and pencils! No, no! Somehow, he would have to score! Some way, he would come back—

Oh, God! I don't know!

What does Scarpa want? Where should Scarpa live? The Waldorf Towers? The best?

Who wanted Baldo Scarpa?

Baldo tried not to think about that. He was free, that was all that mattered. He was going home. He would rest, and eat good food, and smoke cigars, and after a time he would make up his mind—

No good, no good! No fire, no plans, no clear thinking, no connections, no dough! No balls!

Maybe that would all come. Give it time! Give a tired man time! Was sixty-seven that old? He didn't have much of an appetite. The sandwich he bought on the train was expensive, forty cents. In the days Baldo remembered, forty cents had been a lot of money. You could buy a whole meal at some places for forty cents. Now it only got you a ham sandwich.

He didn't have much money. There were his prison earnings, which didn't amount to any great sum, and there was the money they had given him to start over in the world with. With a jolt he realized he would be eligible for social security payments now—except that he had never paid into the fund. He hadn't been interested in such things back then. And, now that he was old and could use the money, he regretted his arrogance, his confidence. He had gone through millions.

It was late afternoon now. The train drew closer to New York. They were travelling through Westchester now, through the neat little suburbs, and then they burst into Manhattan, on the elevated track looking down on the cluttered misery of Harlem. The stop at 125th Street came and went and then Baldo realized this was the end of the journey and in another few minutes he would be at Grand Central.

The train jerked to a stop. Doors clanged open. People began to scramble out. Baldo moved slowly, in no rush to quit the train. He came to his feet, swayed, grabbed the edge of a seat for support. Then he moved out of the train and slowly up the long ramp, looking around for the people who were supposed to meet him.

"Papa!" a voice shrilled. *"Papa!"*

A woman was waving at him from the top of the ramp. Baldo Scarpa squinted uncertainly. Was that Helen? She hadn't even been a woman yet when he went away. Just a skinny girl with long black ringlets and bony legs and a flat chest. And here was this *woman.* She looked like the twin of his dead wife, but slimmer, more American. There was moisture in Baldo's eyes, and he flicked it away angrily.

He could see the others now. Carl was there, as he had promised, and another man, even bigger than Carl, square-chinned and bulky. And a boy of five—

Baldo hurried forward.

"Papa!" Helen cried again as he came near. She threw her arms around him, and he was upset by the vibrant warmth of her, the urgency of her hug. He had to remind himself, after seventeen years of lonely celibacy, that this full-bodied woman embracing him was his daughter.

He stood away.

"Let me look at you," he said. "You're beautiful!"

She was—almost. She had grown tall, and deep breasts swelled against a thin print blouse. The tight skirt gave hint of the wide hips and womanly loins beneath. Her body was ripe, almost voluptuous. Now, as she entered her thirties, she should be in the prime of her beauty.

But there was something wrong about the set of her jaw,

the expression on her lips, the look in her eyes. Something that told Baldo instantly that she was not a happy woman. Was it his return that distressed her? Or was it some lack in her marriage? Always a sharp judge, Baldo decided that it was the latter. This was some long-rankling thing that robbed Helen of the fullest bloom of her beauty. Something that had festered in her over many years.

Her eyes were wet, now, and so were his. "Papa, you know Carl, don't you?" she said.

"Of course. Of course."

"And this is Jim. My husband."

Odd that she should introduce the husband *after* Malfino, Baldo thought. But he turned to the big man and extended a quivering hand. "Pleased to meet you, Jim."

"It's my pleasure, Mr. Scarpa."

"Don't be so formal! Papa!"

"All right—Pop," Keleher said. He was at least six feet three, a solid two-hundred-pounder-plus. Baldo sensed an immediate gulf. Baldo's kind of people were razor-keen, quick on their feet, quick with their wits. And this stolid Irishman was clearly not that sort at all. He was slow-moving and probably slow-thinking as well. A hard worker, though, and a good husband.

"And this is Tommy," Helen was saying. "Give Grandpa a big hug, Tommy."

"I don't want to!" the boy said.

"Tommy!" Helen cried sharply. "What a terrible thing to say!"

"I don't like him. He's old and he looks ugly! Why do I have to have a jailbird for a grandpa anyway?"

There was a moment of silence. Baldo looked about uncertainly. Helen was too embarrassed to react. Jim Keleher had reacted with a foolish, inadvertent smile as though aware of his own incapacity to handle the situation.

It was Carl Malfino who knelt to the boy's level. "Don't talk to your grandpa like that, Tommy," he said in his direct, rapid way. "He's your mommy's daddy, and he loves you. That's not the way to talk to him."

The boy shrugged. "Don't like him."

Malfino glanced up, then came back to the child. "You want me to take you fishing next week?" he demanded. "If you do, you better give your grandpa a big hug."

A moment passed, and then the boy reached up, and as

Baldo stooped down, he received a grudging kiss. Tommy said, "Your whiskers scratch, Grandpa."

Baldo laughed. "What a boy he is!" he exclaimed. "Going to be a giant. Like his papa."

But there wasn't much resemblance, he thought, between Jim and Tommy Keleher. Tommy had none of his father's blocky, robust constitution. Tall the boy was, and handsome, but in a delicate way. Well, time for him to fill out in the years to come.

It was odd, Baldo reflected, that Malfino, not the boy's father, had taken charge of the situation when the boy balked. Malfino had quicker wits than the Irishman, he decided. A glance passed between his daughter and her husband —a glance expressive of strain and an unvoiced tension. A wave of depression settled. Was he the cause of trouble in the little family?

Baldo managed a smile. "Well? What are we gonna do now?"

"Dinner, Papa," Helen said. "Then home. First a good meal, though."

"Don't you cook?"

"Oh, sure," Helen said.

Jim Keleher said, "My idea, Pop! This is supposed to be a celebration."

"Let's go," Malfino said, and left.

Baldo's eyes started out at the prices—a dollar fifty for meatballs and spaghetti! "*Mamma mia*" he grimaced humorously, "I did better in the can! Maybe if I knew this, I wouldn't be in such a hurry to get out."

"Papa," Helen said, lowering her eyes, indicating the hovering waiter. "People are listening."

"I'm not ashamed," Baldo said loudly. "For seventeen years, I keep my nose clean, I don't chisel on my income tax, I don't owe no bills, I leave a good impression—and the governor himself gives me a testimonial. Meanwhile a lot of politicians running around are disgracing the country—"

"Martinis!" Carl Malfino announced, holding up four fingers, "And a glass of milk for the little boy!"

Baldo drank slowly, letting the alcohol sting and warm his palate and throat and settle in his belly. Except for a sort of prune and raisin brandy, distilled by a bootlegging ring of convicts in Clinton Prison, it was his first drink in seventeen

years. Slowly he let his hand caress the thick, white tablecloth and thought of lost years. Then he paused. "Hey, kid,
kid!" he said to Helen.

Helen had tossed a martini off at a gulp.

Malfino caught the glance and laughed. "She's got a wood-
en leg," he laughed, pressing Baldo's arm in a tight grasp.
Malfino drank with relish, huddling over his glass. "Drink
up, Jimsy boy!" he commanded. Keleher slowly raised his
glass and put it down, untouched.

They talked. Weather, baseball, politics. Baldo Scarpa
found himself talking steadily, remorselessly, tirelessly—
bringing out a torrent of information picked up through the
grapevine in the big prison. A Chinese general in Venezuela
was sitting on ten million dollars of Nationalist China gold
located in a Swiss bank. Heroin was flowing into the country from Egypt. A former United States Ambassador had
started a soft drink concession in a Latin American country. An important actress had started out as a prostitute.
And so on and on. But the flow was all one way, and a
moment of silence finally came.

Uncomfortable silence.

Eyes glanced about and sought the tablecloth.

Baldo turned to his son-in-law. "I hear you run a grocery
store, Jim. Does it make out?"

Keleher's big hands were rolling bread into lumps of
dough. "Wholesale grocery, Mr. Scar—Pop," he said de-
precatingly. "I make out. I'm no millionaire."

"Those damn miserable hours!" Helen's voice was slurred.
"Five in the morning he's out! Can you beat that? Sometimes he isn't home till eight, nine o'clock."

"It's business," Keleher muttered.

"This ain't good," Baldo said apprehensively. "You got a
wife, Jim, you got a son, you should spend time with them.
Not all the time working. Why do you think I could take
the cancer?" he demanded grimly. "The time came, I wanted
to put my hand out and feel a woman." He glanced around.
"Yeah, yeah! You can be old, but that stays!" His glance
fell on his grandson. "Let the boy hear me! That's what it
means in the can! Old as you are, you can cry yourself to
sleep, many a night.'"

There was a stir of embarrassment.

"I work for the family," Keleher said. "You can't run
a business part time. I got to put in the time. But it'll show

returns soon. I'll put in some help and take things easier. We'll get a new car, Helen can dress better, we'll make that trip to Florida in the wintertime—"

Helen laughed grimly. "What a pipe dream!" she exclaimed. "We're married six years, and I've been getting that Florida song the last four. Papa, he just likes to work. I think he's queer that way—"

"Shut up," said Carl Malfino quietly. "Just shut up! Your papa's first day back, why chew at each other?"

"Sorry," Helen muttered, half sardonically and half in earnest apology.

Baldo frowned and took another sip of his wine. His thoughts centered on Carl Malfino. They had been pretty good friends in Clinton, but somehow he resented Malfino's presence here. Even if Malfino did come from his old neighborhood in Brooklyn. Even if Malfino had been Helen's suitor six or seven years ago. Baldo had the feeling that Malfino exerted a strange control over both Helen and Jim Keleher. They seemed peculiarly limp and helpless before Carl.

Faced with the complexities of life again after the stark black-and-white prison life, Baldo Scarpa felt a dull ache beginning to grow under his breastbone.

"We're all too jumpy," he said. "We got to relax. We got to enjoy." He finished his wine, and took a coin from his pocket. Pointing to the jukebox, he said to Tommy, "Go put the dime in the slot."

The boy smiled and ran over to carry out the task. A moment later the raucous notes of some current hit boomed out in the restaurant. Baldo smiled. He poured more wine for himself. Helen took the bottle from him and refilled her own glass. It was good wine, ruby-red Valpolicella. Helen drinks too much, Baldo thought.

Helen said, "We got a place all fixed up for you, papa. We had this extra room that Jim used for storage, and now we got a bed in there and a chest of drawers and everything."

"I didn't want you to go to much trouble for me," Baldo said mildly.

"Trouble? What's trouble? For your own father? You'll like it, papa. And I'm a good cook, believe it or not. You got to taste my lasagne. It's as good as Mama's, positive! It—something the matter, papa?"

"Nothing," Baldo said, turning his head to one side. The mention of lasagne—of his wife, dead these thirteen years—they hadn't even let him out to go to her funeral—

A dark bitter voice said inside him, Baldo Scarpa wants to cry! Just a weepy old man, that's what you are now. Your daughter says lasagne and you go all to pieces.

He got control of himself. Carl told a joke, spelling out the punch line to keep it from Tommy, and they all laughed. The atmosphere began to change, to grow less tense. It was the wine, Baldo knew. It was melting Jim's reserve, it was breaking down the coolness in Helen. They ordered a second bottle. Baldo refused to have any. After all these years, too much to drink the first day would make him sick. Helen drank most of his share.

When the meal was over, Baldo tried to take the check. He grasped at it, got it from the waiter, and said, "This is my treat." He was stunned to find, upon turning it over, that it came to close to thirty dollars. But he intended to pay it anyway.

He had his wallet half out of his pocket when Carl Malfino tossed three tens and a five on the table and said, "That ought to take care of it, Baldo. Come on, everybody. Let's clear out."

"No, no," Baldo insisted. He tried to shove the money across the table to Malfino.

"Let Carl take the check, Papa," Helen whispered into Baldo's ear. "He can afford it. You've got to be careful about spending your money."

"Careful? Who? I never been careful in my life," Baldo said. "This is Baldo Scarpa!"

"This *was* Baldo Scarpa!" Helen corrected.

Father and daughter exchanged glances.

"You think I'm a bum?" Baldo demanded.

"No, Papa!"

Baldo made a Latin gesture. "I'm gonna pay you rent!" he said strongly. "I'm gonna carry my weight. I just need a little time—I'm just as good as I was!"

"Who wants rent?" Helen cried.

Malfino broke in and placed the check before Baldo Scarpa with a gesture of invitation. "Okay, Mr. Scarpa! It's a matter of respect. Your treat, this time."

Baldo took a breath. "Okay," he announced. "Okay! Maybe I should of kept my big mouth shut!" he added humorously, and everyone laughed. He had to admit, Carl Malfino had a way.

In the waiting car, Baldo looked at Jim in perplexity. "No gear shift?"

"Automatic, Pop," Keleher said.

"I been away a long time," Baldo decided, fingering an empty wallet. Keleher drove down Second Avenue, turning off at 10th Street into a shabby block, but one house was less shabby than the others. It was with some relief that Baldo saw Jim pull up in front of that one and announce, "Here we are!"

They got out. Jim said to Carl Malfino, "You want me to drive you to the subway, Carl?"

"Don't be silly. It's only a few blocks." Turning, Malfino scooped Tommy up high into the air, put him down, and said, "Is it a date for fishing next weekend?"

"It's a date, Uncle Carl!"

"Right. Well, thanks for a swell day, Jim, Helen. And welcome back, Baldo. I'll be talking to you pretty soon." He shook Baldo's hand, then Jim's, then took Helen's and held it for a moment without shaking it, in a gesture of unusual warmth. With a last wave at everyone, Malfino walked away toward the corner.

They went upstairs. The Keleher family lived on the third floor in a walk-up building. They had a small, extremely neat little apartment, four rooms, all tiny. The room set aside for him was the smallest of the four. It just barely was big enough for the narrow bed and the few pieces of second-hand furniture. But that was all right, Baldo thought. He had a roof over his head. He didn't need a palace.

It was late at night, past ten. Tommy, up way past his bedtime, was asleep on his feet. Jim Keleher was yawning too. Baldo felt wearied by the long train ride and the hectic dinner, but he knew he would get little sleep tonight. His brain was too active, whirring with the excitement of being free. Over the empty years, behind bars, he had dreamt himself to sleep on his cot, dreaming of this moment, and more than once the prison pillow had been wet with tears. But this was not what he had expected. Undercurrents of foreboding. All was not well between Helen and her husband. Where was the sense of confidence? They were cold toward him—was it fear? Why not? he thought somberly.

The jailbird had come home. The man of crime. The doer of evil. A grim smile tugged at the powerful mouth.

Baldo unpacked his suitcase and laid out his belongings—shirt, underwear, socks, a bible given by the chaplain, toothbrush, a cigarette box made of matches. Too tired to undress, he sat and looked at the wall, wondering how it felt to be free. When was that feeling supposed to come?

When Helen entered, she was dressed for bed, the heavy-bodied ripeness visible under the nightgown.

"Everything all right, Papa?"

Baldo looked up. "I can remember when *I* put *you* to bed."

"Oh, Papa!" Helen said uncomfortably.

Baldo nodded. "Sure, sure! Don't mind me. All set for sleep?"

Helen sat down and lit a cigarette.

"You smoke?" Baldo asked.

"Oh, sure!" Helen replied.

"Why not go to your husband?" Baldo demanded.

"Him?" The woman's eyes under the harsh electric light were encircled with scorn. "The man's out snoring like a pig before he hits the blanket. In the middle of the night—up and out to the store!" Helen shook her head. "At least, Papa, you'll be around the house."

"Eh," said Baldo.

"What does that mean?" she demanded.

Baldo shrugged. "You see a lot of Carl?"

Helen glanced up, and then away. "Not too much," she shrugged. "He lives in Brooklyn, you know. Works in a church. What makes you ask?"

"No reason," Baldo replied. "Only this church—"

"What's wrong with a church?"

"I would feel better if he was digging ditches."

"Hey? What?"

"It would be more natural. A church sounds like a scheme. I don't like the smell."

Helen stared deep into her father's fierce eyes, sensing depths of sadness she could not fathom. She looked away. "Carl's all right," she muttered. "At least he's a man. Good night, Papa—" she arose and found her hand caught in a massive, ropy hand.

"Not even a kiss?" Baldo asked.

"Sorry, Papa!" She bent over to kiss him, and the carbolic

smell of prison soap, still clinging, was not unpleasant. And then he held her back, his grip tightening.

"What, Papa?"

"You're using perfume?" Baldo demanded. "For who? For what? For this man who's out snoring? A decent Catholic woman—"

"Papa!" Helen cried. "I use the perfume for me! I like to walk with a nice smell. What's wrong?"

Baldo was staring, working his mouth with anger, suffused with an old rage. Why? Where had the feeling come from? Why was he shaking? This was his daughter—full-breasted, grown, who drank too much and had creases under her eyes, but who had once sat on his knee. "Go away," he said thickly.

"What's wrong?"

Baldo turned away. "Nothing," he muttered. "Nothing to worry your head. Crazy things go through an old jailbird's head. Baldo Scarpa. Baldo Scarpa!" he muttered.

"I'll turn out the light?" she suggested.

"Good night," he said in a low voice. *"Bambina mia!"*

He lay in darkness, wondering at the fear in his daughter's eyes—fear of a man who would give his life for flesh of his flesh. When he drifted into sleep, his thoughts, he reflected, were still those of prison days and prison nights. What had the perfume triggered off? Baldo could fool anybody but—Baldo.

Inside, Baldo Scarpa knew!

In his first days of freedom, Baldo Scarpa stayed close to home. He woke at five out of habit, with the sound of his son-in-law's bathroom noises, and then he remained in bed, staring into the past, until Helen began to stir at seven.

Down to the corner for a newspaper, no further. Then stand at the corner and watch the children—children whose parents had been children when he had gone into the big house. Then stare at the tail-finned automobiles, and the housing projects, and back to Helen's house. Helen's house! In the past it had been Baldo's house—

Hey, Baldo Scarpa! Just outa the can—
Tommy's grandpa! Killed a lot of men—
Still looks mean, don't he—?
Why'd they let him out—?
Cancer—
Why pick our block to live—?
A lot of respect for a man like that—

A mixed bag of reactions, he thought wryly. No one knew how to treat the freak! Big man or bum—take your pick! He felt out of place in Manhattan. He had spent most of his life across the river in Brooklyn, where things were quiet; you could see trees, small houses with lawns. Here it was all tenements and housing projects—worse than jail, he thought! No space to turn around. Across the greasy river he could see Brooklyn Heights—old friends, associates, kindness, and danger. He had taken three falls with the law. A fourth fall, and it was the hole forever!

The days passed in suffering. The noises outside, the fire engines wailing past, the kids screaming at stickball all brought him up sweating—all pressed in on him. When would he again take the world in stride?

"Hey, kid, what's wrong? he demanded.

Helen was ironing. "Nothing, Papa. What should be wrong?"

"Jim works too hard. Why? He's got some reason? He comes home late, sure! Then a quick meal, and by ten asleep. No television? No radio? And away in the morning? Six days a week! And Sundays he sleeps around the clock? When?"

Helen glanced up with the iron hissing steam gently. "When what?" she asked cynically.

"Eh, you know?" Baldo said uncomfortably. "I'm embarrassed to talk!"

Helen held the iron to her cheek. "I'm a married woman, Papa! I know all you know, and maybe a little more. While you've been away, I've had an education. What would you want?"

Baldo held up a finger. "A little noise in the next room," he said seriously. "I want to hear that bedspring. I want to hear some whisper. I want a man making love to a woman. A man with a man, I saw enough of that in the can. Why is the man running from a real woman?"

Helen touched a finger to her tongue, then to the iron,

listening to the quick splat of noise. "Mama used to tell me, you got to bring the thread to the needle. Not the needle to the thread."

"She was a saint in heaven," Baldo said seriously.

"In heaven is right," Helen replied. "Maybe she's looking down on this marriage."

Baldo sat thinking deeply.

"And on the marriage night, your mama, looking down, did she see blood on the sheets?"

Helen's glance was cool and thoughtful and edged with anger. "I got a lot of work, Papa. Why don't you take Tommy down to the park. When I want you to know, I'll run up a red flag."

Carl Malfino was a frequent visitor. He came on Friday evening, and again on Saturday afternoon, and on Sunday he went fishing with Tommy while Jim slept and Helen mended clothes. He was bold and confident.

Baldo opened the door for him on Sunday. "I can wake Jim up," he said uncertainly.

"Let him sleep," Carl replied confidently. "I got some ideas I want to take up with Helen."

"What ideas?"

"Should I ask my parole officer for permission to get married!" Carl Malfino burst into laughter and sought Helen out in the small living room where he talked vigorously, argumentatively, familiarly. After a time, Helen's laughter rang out.

Baldo went into the bedroom. "Jim—"

"Huh?"

"Malfino's outside. Talking with Helen. Don't you want to join the party?"

"Huh? Uh. No. No, Pop! Let me sleep—"

"Wake up, Jim!"

The giant hulk turned on the creaking bed. "For cris sake, Pop! I work hard. I need my sleep. Stop pulling at me—"

"But Malfino—"

"What about Malfino?"

"All right! Sleep, you thick mick!" Baldo stalked back to his own bedroom, skirting the living room where a bottle of wine stood on the table; he huddled over the small television set, watching the dots race before his eyes. Just after his conviction for armed robbery, Carl Malfino had sought him out in Clinton Prison, in the big yard, bold and confident with the swagger of a big man. "I'm Carl Malfino," he said. "I was supposed to marry your daughter."

"Why tell me?" Baldo had said stiffly.

"I thought you'd want to know," Malfino replied, disconcerted.

Baldo stared about the desolate yard, freezing in the winter cold of the Adirondacks. "You're a con!" he said flatly. "A criminal! I'm glad you didn't score!"

Malfino flushed with rage. "You old bastard!" he cried, and then the guard was stalking past, swinging his stick, and they parted. Not long after came a letter announcing that Helen had married a young man with an Irish name. And soon after a picture announcement of the birth of a son named Thomas. And then a long silence.

Whose son was it? Baldo wondered.

He found himself talking back to the television set. Eh! Baldo Scarpa! Baldo Scarpa! A big man, good-looking, strong face—and his insides were chewed away. Somebody had dirtied his doorstep and inside—nothing! No rage, no strength, no saving reservoirs of anger to deal with the polluter! Not even a son to take action. Nothing, nothing, nothing but the fear of the big house! In that moment he hated all the Irish!

He found the telephone book and began to look up old names.

A receptionist with harlequin glasses and a bosom beyond belief said, "Can I help you, sir?"

She saw a tall, fierce man with hard features, dignified and self-contained, not too different from the sort of men she was accustomed to admit.

"You tell Mr. Spallaccio that Mr. Scarpa is here."

The girl looked doubtful. "Do you have an appointment?"

"Tell Mr. Spallaccio it's Mr. Scarpa."

"One moment!" The girl plugged in a jack and talked for a moment and her expression changed. She said, "Mr. Spallaccio will see you at once. There's a boy on his way to show you in."

Moments later Baldo was led through an immense expanse of bottling works where highly automated machinery was filling, capping, and labeling bottles with a well-known brand name. An elevator rose slowly to an upper floor where he

was led past rows of quiet, fluorescent-lit desks where billing and shipping went on in a hum of tabulating machinery.
Baldo was dumbfounded. Nothing on the outside had ad-
justed him to the immense changes which had overtaken
the liquor industry.

The door read:

NICHOLAS J. SPALLACCIO, PRESIDENT.

"Come in, Baldo!" sang out a gay, hoarse voice.

Nick Spallaccio wore a sleek two-hundred-dollar suit and
a large diamond ring on a manicured finger. Over the years
he had gained weight and his hair had gone white. Baldo
felt a qualm of inferiority sink through his belly. He waited
gravely, conscious that his footing was uncertain. Spallaccio
came forward with a financier's handshake—warm, strong,
quick, formal. Baldo squared his shoulders.

"Great to see you again, Baldo!" Spallaccio said in a
hoarse, familiar voice. "How long is it? Eighteen years?
Sit down, man! Drink?" He turned to a teakwood bar
"What about a Scotch?"

"Your brand, Nick?"

Spallaccio chuckled with an air of complacency. "A distillery here, a distillery there. Comes in handy. You can
taste the heather. We own a piece of the shipping line. Here!"

Baldo put it down at a gulp and found himself squeezing
back tears of smooth fire. He found himself noting details: expensive carpeting, a wood-burning fireplace, blond
wood paneling, an oil painting—extremely lush, extremely
naked and explicit. He turned back to face a satisfied, quiet
smile across an expanse of desk quite clear of paper. An
electronic air purifier was humming.

"A long way since '43," Baldo observed.

Spallaccio glanced at pink fingernails. "I got a wonderful son-in-law who's my tax adviser, Baldo," he grinned.
"Harvard School of Business. I'm a grandpapa four times."

"I'm a grandpapa once," Baldo said.

"Give it time," Spallaccio observed. "Wonderful girl—
Helen. How's she getting on?"

"Fine!" Baldo waited. "Have I got time?"

"Hey? What?"

Baldo looked up gravely. "They took a lot of time out
of my life," he observed. "How much is left?"

Spallaccio stared, sobered, and then snapped his fingers.
"Forget it, Baldo! You're out! You look good in that sun-

burn! You got your health! It's what counts! Another
Scotch?"

"Sure!" Baldo felt warmer and to his surprise something
within was quaking. He raised his voice. "I hear the business
is grossing past fifty million, Nick?"

Spallaccio chuckled, but his eyes had gone watchful.
"Publicity, Baldo! We got a guy, Meaney, an Irish, king of
Broadway, plants that stuff with the columns. Actually, we
got to skip a dividend this year."

"Yeah?"

"We're in a profit squeeze. Question of taxes."

"I been hearing mergers talk with that mob in Toronto."

"Just a tax loss we're buying."

"What's a tax loss?"

Spallaccio lit a fat cigar, pushed over a pre-Castro box
of Havanas. "It's hard to explain, Baldo. I got to ask my
other son-in-law." He glanced at a thin Swiss watch. "In
eighteen years, a lot of things change, Baldo. I keep three firms
of lawyers working on problems." He glanced up coldly
through drifting smoke. "I got an understanding with the
Treasury people. I keep a clean operation, I'm religious
about my tax. You got no idea how many kinds of tax
bites hit the industry—"

"Over and under the table?"

Spallaccio finished the cigar in a long thoughtful silence
pregnant with meaning. He was staring at a plume of
greasy smoke climbing over a biscuit factory in Long Island City. Neither cared to break the silence. Neither was
called on to comment.

Spallaccio broke the silence. "Baldo, I don't ask how
you get on with the parole board, do I?"

"No."

"Don't ask how I get on with the Treasury. I got daughters married off to professional men—a lawyer, an accountant. Two daughters with the nuns. One little girl going to
marry into artichokes. I get invited to yacht parties by
these Greek shipping people and I put money in plays
where nobody asks what kind of bums I feel sorry for.
Eighteen years is a long time. I lost a boy in Korea, to be
truthful, and I keep thinking about my good name."

Baldo stared grimly. He was thinking of the day when
the distance between Spallaccio's throat and his own powerful fingers would long since have closed. Inside he felt

nothing but a sad, cold wonder at himself. Spallaccio's piggish eyes had taken his measure.

"Am I a bum?" Baldo asked.

Spallaccio smoked thoughtfully. "Yeah, I think so," he said finally. "You look good to the outside, Baldo. That long rest done you good but that sunburn—it shows you're sitting on park benches. And another thing—"

"Yeah?"

"It's taking you too long to come out with it." Spallaccio delicately broke off an ash. "You're here for something. I'm waiting. Spallaccio waits—and Scarpa can't get to spit it out." A cold, estimated smile twisted the fat mouth. "What's on your mind, Baldo?"

Baldo waited for a surge of rage that failed to come. He lowered his eyes, staring at his strong hands, then looked up grimly. "A job?"

"What of job?"

"Vice-president." Baldo hesitated, and added, "At least."

Spallaccio's smile widened. "Of what?"

"I know the business."

"Yeah?" Spallaccio swiveled, spoke quietly into an instrument. A secretary brought in a thick volume running to fifteen hundred pages, and left. Spallaccio riffled the pages— rules and regulations affecting and governing the liquor industry. "You don't know one page."

"I give you this company when I was sent up."

Spallaccio shook his head. "I *bought* this company when you was sent up," he corrected grimly. "For taxes I bought it—and it was nothing, an old bootleg outfit with nothing but a label. In hock to the mob. I took it. I made it. You got paid off."

"I could buy back."

"With what? Your left leg?" Spallaccio's fat face had become ugly. Suddenly, he forced a smile and drew a chair to face the gaunt giant. "Could you take a selling job?"

Baldo shook his head.

"I got a spot in shipping and billing. You could handle that at ninety bucks a week and fringe benefits—"

"You think Baldo Scarpa can work for fringe benefits?"

Spallaccio nodded. "Be reasonable, Baldo! It's all you're good for. You know and I know!"

"No."

Spallaccio rose with an expression of regret. "I won't

argue, Baldo. I got a—let's see!" He hesitated over the word. "—A corporate responsibility. It ain't the money. Personally, I can let you have—" he examined an alligator-skin billfold and dumped the contents—"three thousand. Call it a loan. Pay when you like."

Baldo turned the bills over curiously. "If I took one cent, Nick," he said gravely, "I'd be a bum, wouldn't I?"

Spallaccio nodded. "Yeah."

"In my place, Nick, what would you do?"

Spallaccio sat back thoughtfully. "I would kill Nick Spallaccio," he grunted.

Baldo went to the door. "But you never did seventeen years," he said sardonically. "It's the difference, Nick! Seventeen years! I'll come back and buy you. Thank you for your time." Striking his biceps, he struck a fist in the air in an ancient gesture, and left.

"Baldo Scarpa!" Spallaccio murmured.

After a moment, he spat with disgust and dialed a number.

"Mr. Northrup?"

Harry Northrup swung about with an alert expression. In Manhattan. "Yes Nick?"

"I couldn't give him that job, and he wouldn't take money. I didn't think he would," Spallaccio advised. "Personally, I don't think he's fit for anything."

"Maybe, maybe not," Northrup murmured, and hung up. A fresh, up-to-date picture of Baldo Scarpa, as he looked on the day of his release from Clinton Prison, sat on the desk before him, flanked by photographs of a group of South American personalities. He lit a cigarette and continued to work until late in the night on voluminous reports supplied by a variety of Federal law enforcement agencies on the precarious structure of the country in question.

Through the curling smoke of a cigar, he was studying the old creased report of a robbery, an armed robbery which had sent Carl Malfino to the prison at Dannemora.

10

Baldo sat trembling aboard a Manhattan-bound express train, conscious of tearing eyes and an empty feeling. It was the old story. Everybody was out for himself. He felt like a fool, as though seventeen years at Clinton Prison, an insitution of advanced studies in human behavior, had taught him nothing of the realities. He could hardly blame Nick Spallaccio. He had handled the whole thing wrong. He had come, cap in hand, a beggar, a blind man with a tin cup, crawling for crumbs—instead of working through top connections.

Top connections? What top connections? A sad, wry smile twisted his gaunt features. Nick Spallaccio had thrown chicken feed at him and the chicken refused to peck. It was a laugh, but oddly comforting. The money could have bought—what? A shadow crossed his face. At least rent to Helen and Jim and a small legacy in savings bonds for Tommy's education. Suddenly, delayed rage overtook him—but rage at himself, rage at his failures, his weaknesses, his inability to overcome the residues of stupid, inappropriate pride long enough to leave property to his grandson.

As the train roared through the tunnel under the East River, he buried his face in his hands and fought back bitter tears, and then his mind ran on.

What else to do? There was the old bunch out there in Brooklyn. Macalusco ran a bowling alley now. And a piece of *bolito* on the side, Malfino had said. Lupo, Arcari—no, those two were dead or disappeared. Little Augie? Goldie Feinberg? Jackson, Bobo Nagel? The whole pack were dead or in prison.

He was alone.

He got off at 59th Street and walked down to a hotel on Park Avenue where flags of foreign diplomats were hung. He passed under a green and white flag with three stars in the center and found himself in an empty barroom. Forbidden territory, but he could take a chance.

"Beer."

He sat nursing the pale brew, untasted, as the bar man polished glasses.

"Frank show up any more?"

The bar man turned. "Frank who?"

"Uncle Frank?"

"Who's asking?"

"Nobody."

The bar man turned back to his task. "He's in Leavenworth," he said briefly. "Don't you read?"

"Oh, sure, sure! I forgot." Baldo sipped the beer, feeling

scrutinized and uncomfortable. "Does anybody know how Lucky's doing?"

"I wouldn't know, Mister!"

"Bum rap—Lucky! He was never involved."

The bar man paused. "Why are we talking Lucky?"

"No reason."

"He's been away a long time."

"A long time," Baldo murmured thoughtfully, and then it all seemed pointless. He turned and left through the rich lobby of remembered luxury. The Manhattan telephone book was thicker than he ever remembered. He turned finally to the Bronx book.

"Hello?"

"Rosa? Rosa, this is Baldo."

"I'll connect you with the boss," the voice said. Baldo waited, then a woman's voice came. "Hello, who's this?"

"Baldo."

"Baldo who?"

"Baldo Scarpa."

A moment's pause, and then, to his relief, a voice cried out in pleasure, "No! This some sort of joke?"

"Big joke. I'm out, Rosa. I'm living with my daughter."

"Jeez, can you beat that? Baldo Scarpa!"

"Look, can I come see you today?"

"Sure. Any time. You know how to get here?"

"All I got is the address. I don't know the Bronx."

She told him the instructions, twice. He repeated them to her, and continued to repeat them to himself as he boarded the uptown train.

It was a long trip, nearly an hour. He left the station and walked up the sun-baked, hilly street where Rosa lived. Apartment 3-C, she said. He rode the ancient elevator up. Rosa Amato, he thought! He had met her in 1936, the first time. She was just under thirty, then, and he was in his forties and vigorous. A chorus girl at one of the 42nd Street strip-joints, a dark-eyed, dark-haired girl with ripe hips and high, jutting breasts. For seven years she had been his mistress, confidante, and the most important person in the world to him. When La Guardia closed down the strip joints, she needed another job, and he had found her one in Brooklyn. Near where he lived. And he had visited her almost nightly, during those years of his power's last flourish.

He knocked. The door opened. Baldo saw into a shabby

apartment. Three girls were sitting behind desks, typing away busily. For the first moment Baldo hardly noticed the middle-aged woman who had opened the door.

Rosa Amato.

More powerfully than anything else, the sight of her bore in on him with smashing impact the passage of the years. She was gray-haired and fat. The exciting fullness of her breasts had turned to pendulous overabundance. Her hips were enormous. A hooked nose jutted out between fleshy cheeks. Only in the darkness of her eyes was there some hint of the beautiful girl of a quarter of a century ago.

"Baldo!"

"Hello, Rosa." He had to struggle to keep from letting his reaction show. "Been a long time."

"Close to twenty years. Come on in, will you?"

The typing didn't cease. Baldo looked at the girls, then at Rosa, and said, "What's this you're running here? Some new kind of cathouse?" He forced a broad smile.

"Called a secretarial service," Rosa said. "I take in typing. Manuscripts, mimeographed bulletins, the works."

"What do you know about being a secretary?"

"I learned, Baldo, I learned. You think I still got the shape to be a stripper?"

"I—I didn't think—"

"Well, I did. I took a secretarial course in '48. Then I set up in business. Now I got too much business for one person, so I hire people. I stay ahead. But come on into my room. Let's have a drink. Old times' sake."

She led him into her bedroom, at the back of the rambling apartment. How many times had he gone into Rosa's bedroom? His heart was suddenly beating with dread.

Rosa took a bottle of sherry from a cupboard and poured out drinks. Rosa had always loved good sherry, Baldo remembered, and the stuff was still good.

"So," she said, smiling. "How does it feel?"

"It's all right," he said without enthusiasm. He sat limply on the edge of the bed, lifting the creases of his trousers.

"You look good," she said appreciatively. "That suit fits. You had a long rest?"

He smiled wanly, thinking that Rosa's enthusiasms had been her good point. "A long rest," he agreed, and lifted his glass for a refill. *"Salute!"*

"Salute!"

They drank, smiling at each other, old friends conscious of the years.

"And you, Rosa?"

Her dark eyes twinkled. "A good drink, a roll in the hay, I'm still Rosa, but now I'm a little fat. How's the wife?"

"A long time dead."

"Oh, sure, sure!" Rosa smacked her forehead. "I ought to cut my tongue out. And the little girl—the one you used to give all my kewpie dolls from the dressing room? What's her name? Edith?"

"Helen."

"Oh, yeah, yeah! She's married?"

Baldo's smile was troubled. "Five-year-old boy."

"I'll bet he's the spittin' image of his old man!"

Baldo shrugged. "Of *this* old man," he said somberly, tapping his chest. "The boy's old man is an Irish. But the child don't look Irish."

"Eh?"

Baldo blinked and looked up. "Nothing." More small talk, and Rosa refilled the wine glasses. There was an interruption, and a girl entered with a question about punctuation. Rosa made introductions—Kim Feigenbaum and Mr. Scarpa. The girl smiled at the tall, distinguished, rather frightening old man and left, enlightened on the use of the semi-colon. Rosa smiled crookedly.

"She's no lay, Baldo," she advised. "A nice girl, but she can't spell. I could get you a girl."

Baldo wet his lips. "I'm too old to cut the mustard, Rosa. A kid like that, not for me."

"You, old?" she scoffed. "Give me five minutes."

Baldo glanced at his watch. "I had a hard day, Rosa. Maybe I can come back?"

"Oh, sure, sure!" Rosa got up, still smiling. "I got to remember I can't fool around in working hours," she added good-humoredly. "If my accountant taught me one thing it is this: I dassn't eat up my overhead. Any time you need action, give me a half-hour's notice."

"I'll call next week," Baldo promised falsely.

"Any time," Rosa sang. "And forget that old man talk! You're still a sight for sore eyes, Baldo. A real man, a real man!"

Baldo left, smiling without mirth, and on the street, he mopped his neck of cold sweat, surprised that he was left shaking by the encounter. The young girl had frightened him by the perfume of her presence—the same shaking induced by Helen's perfume that first night. He was afraid—afraid to put himself to the test. In the lonely years at Clinton Prison he had fought off deprivation. Once or twice he had relieved himself in the dark, but the dirty business had left him with a soiled feeling and he had disciplined himself against everything but a prisoner's dreams. And now he was shaking—impotent, emasculated. Had he gone queer in those years?

The recurrent thought left him in the grip of terror. What was a man without a woman? What was Baldo Scarpa? Had the years taken all his manhood? He had come to test himself on Rosa—and then, at the thought of a creased belly and baggy breasts, something within him of imagined desire had died. Had it been there in the first place?

No, no good, no good! he thought desperately. He would better have been left in the big prison set in the frozen hills of the north.

On the subway a young woman rose and offered him her seat. At his shouted refusal she looked frightened and got off at the next stop.

Helen opened the door with a worried look. Her hands and face were smudged with flour. "Oh, Papa!" she said with relief. "There was a call for you. Somebody from the district attorney's office. It's not trouble?"

"Trouble?" Baldo frowned. "Who called?"

"A man named Mr. Northrup. He'll be there till six. He wants you to call back."

"I see."

Baldo entered the little apartment and got a hug from Tommy who was playing with paper cowboys and Indians on the kitchen table. Helen followed, wiping flour on her skirt. "What does he want, Papa?"

"Who?"

"Mr. Northrup," she said tightly. "He's not going to send you back?"

Baldo glanced at his grandson who was firing a cap pistol at the paper figures. "Nobody's going to send me back. Not ever," he said grimly. He carefully put aside his hat. "He wants me for a stool. Only I got nothing to stool about. If he calls again, I didn't come back."

"You got to call him, Papa!"

"No!"

"If you don't, I will, and he'll send dectectives here!" she cried. "You're in their hands, Papa! You got to do what they say, not what you want."

"No!" Baldo said stubbornly. "Let him find another stool!"

"I'll call!"

Some moments later, Helen held out the receiver of a telephone. "Find out what he wants, Papa! You can't live like this! Meanwhile, I'll finish the *gnocchi!*"

Baldo picked up the telephone. "Hello?"

Northrup glanced at the hearing piece of his telephone. The harsh voice was unexpectedly discouraged. And sad. He added a burnt-out cigar to a heaped ashtray.

"How does it feel, Baldo?"

"All right," the voice acknowledged cautiously. "I'm out and that's something. You want something?"

"I was expecting to hear from you, Baldo."

"I got nothing to say, Mr. Northrup. I mean that respectfully but there's no reason to call."

"Could you have lunch with me?"

"When?"

"Tomorrow. Any time. Your convenience."

"I don't think so, Mr. Northrup. And another thing," the voice added with reproach, "I don't think it's a nice thing to be calling my home. My daughter gets upset."

"Should I send a cop?" Northrup asked grimly.

"No, but don't upset my daughter."

Northrup waited with a sense of exasperation. This was not going well. "I don't want it put in writing either," he said with impatience. "You recall our talk up at Dannemora?"

"I remember, yes! But I can't work for you. I am my own man. I will live my own life."

"Baldo—" Northrup said, drumming the desk. "Stop thinking along one line. I'm telling you something for your own good. I want you to think about that daughter you claim you're so worried about."

"What?"

Northrup glanced up with a grim smile at Joe Scott who was teetering on a chair with the *Law Journal.* "That drew blood," he advised, covering the mouthpiece. He came back, "I'm talking about Malfino. He's been around a lot, hasn't he?"

A long silence took place. "He visits," the voice said slowly. "The man works. He keeps out of trouble."

"Are you sure?"

Baldo looked around. Helen was banging the stove in the kitchen, making noises to indicate that she was not eavesdropping. He kept his voice low.

"I'm sure."

"Will you think it over?" Northrup demanded.

"Yeah, I'll think," Baldo said.

"You can always call me," Northrup said. "And Baldo?"

"Yeah."

"You keep a tight mouth?"

"I always have."

"Because in my opinion one of these days Carl is going to make a move against that son-in-law of yours. Or inveigle him in something. You'd better have me for a friend than an enemy."

"I don't know what you're talking about, Mr. Northrup. Look, can I hang up now without being disrespectful?"

"Call me when you need me."

"Maybe so, Mr. Northrup. Goodbye."

"Thanks anyway, Baldo."

Baldo Scarpa put down the phone. He frowned. Northrup suspected Carl was up to something, did he? Baldo felt dark forebodings. He wished Malfino did not play so prominent a part in the Keleher family picture. Maybe Northrup was right, that Carl was brewing something. Carl had hinted as much when he visited the prison.

Baldo's shoulders slumped. He did not want to get involved in any of Carl's schemes, if schemes they were. Nor did he want Carl to break up his daughter's marriage. But he did not want to help Northrup, either.

He just wanted life to be simple. Why did it have to be this complicated? Why did he have to live with the pressures that had descended on him? If Northrup would go away, and Carl Malfino too, and just let Helen and Jim and the boy be happy, Baldo would be happy too. As it stood now, he was helpless, unable to act. He could only sit tight and hope that no harm would come to those he loved.

He walked into the kitchen. "What did he want with you?" Helen asked.

"Nothing," Baldo said. "Just checking."

"Anything important?"
"Nothing."

Harry Northrup stared at his thick, powerful fingers and wondered whether or not he had made a fatal blunder by overplaying a weak hand.

He had been waiting so many weeks. And nothing had happened. Now Baldo had been free a whole week, and no hints. The detectives who checked on Malfino's comings and goings had reported frequent visits to the Keleher home. Presumably he was approaching Baldo Scarpa and offering to bring him in on the cocaine operation.

Presumably.

Northrup wondered. In making the phone call, he had gambled everything on two uncertainties: that Malfino had approached Baldo, and that Baldo would cooperate with the law. Baldo had *sounded* sincere in his denial of complicity in any possible Malfino schemes. But Baldo Scarpa was a cagey old man. He knew how to lie.

Northrup had to cling to the belief that Baldo Scarpa's basic motivation was a desire to die outside prison walls. Given that, he had reason to hope the old man might help him against Malfino. The risks of a fourth conviction would surely be too big for Baldo to chance.

Yet suppose Baldo's hatred of the law still overbalanced his fear of conviction? He might turn to Malfino, then. He might at least tip Malfino off that the law knew of his activities, of his contacts with the Morales bunch. And then the job of putting together a case would be ten times as hard.

Northrup realized he was in the uncomfortable position of an angler who had cast his last bit of bait and had it taken. From here on in, he would have to fish with a bare hook and hope for luck. He cursed himself for his impatience. If only he had waited a few more days! Given Malfino enough time to make his pitch to Baldo!

Even so, Baldo might be too stubborn, too proud to co-operate. No way of telling.

Northrup's nerves were drawn tight. This case was dragging on and on, the *Balthazar* sitting quietly like a keg of dynamite, and he had no power to move. Harry Northrup didn't like playing a passive role. He wanted Malfino to hurry up and make a move that could be countered. And he feared for Baldo Scarpa and for Scarpa's family.

He left his office half an hour early, stopped off for a drink, and drove morosely home. He and Donna were attending a dinner party tonight at the home of a television director she knew. Northrup hoped the topics of discussion would stay far away from crime and its prevention. He had the notion that he was going to be less than scintillating tonight.

Baldo Scarpa lay in his narrow bed with his eyes closed, pretending to be asleep and hoping the pretense would somehow be transformed into reality. But his mind was active, driving sleep away. His brain was full of the words of Harry Northrup. He could practically see the assistant district attorney standing at the foot of his bed. There was Northrup now, the short man with the wide shoulders, the crooked nose, the tangle of curly hair, the close-set, inexorable eyes. He stood there like a rock, his jaws clamped tight, his expression rigid.

What did Northrup mean, that Carl was dangerous to Helen and Jim? That didn't make any sense. Carl didn't want any harm to come to the Kelehers.

"He's a dangerous man to have around the house, Baldo," the image of Northrup seemed to be saying. "He's involved in rackets up to his ears. He even uses the church for a cover to make deals. If you let him, he'll drag you in, Baldo. He'll drag you and Helen and Jim and Tommy. That's the kind of a man he is."

He won't hurt any of us! Baldo retorted silently.

"How can you be sure?" the ghostly form of Northrup asked. "You know what sort of man Carl Malfino is, because you were that sort yourself once. Thirty years ago, Baldo. What happened to Benny Rizzo? Wasn't he a friend of yours, Baldo? Didn't you visit his family like an uncle? Tickle his kids under the chin? Where's Benny Rizzo now?

Dead. Dead with his head blown off by a submachine gun. By his good old pal Baldo Scarpa."

That was different! He was a doublecrosser!

"He was a friend, Baldo. You killed him."

How do you know? You were a kid then, Northrup!

"And what about Mike Fucci? Who did *he* doublecross? He was just in your way, Baldo. He had four kids, but he was in your way, so you put a knife in his ribs."

You can't know that! Nobody knows that!

"I know a lot about you, Baldo."

You aren't even here! You're just a trick of my mind, Northrup. I'm a little stir-crazy, that's all. You aren't here. Go away! Go away and let me get some sleep!

"Just remember what I tell you, Baldo. Malfino is hard and cold and all death. Don't trust him. Don't let him get you in a position where you can't resist him."

The apparition of Northrup was gone. Baldo Scarpa sat up, his pajamas drenched with sweat, sticking to his skin. It was a hot, muggy May night. His eyeballs throbbed. His throat was dry.

He heard voices. Coming through the thin plaster partition that separated his room from Helen's and Jim's. They were awake, in there. Having an argument.

Baldo cocked his good ear and listened.

It was Helen who was doing most of the talking. She was saying, "Jim, you've got to speak to him. Tell him we don't want him around the house any more."

"I can't do that, Helen."

"You've got to. It—Lord, do I have to draw pictures for you? I don't like the guy. He gives me the creeps. I wish he wouldn't come around here any more, that's all. And you're the one who's got to tell him."

"I can't do a thing like that. He's my friend, Helen. For years and years. How can I just say, stop bothering us and don't come around?"

"Because I want you to."

"You never used to talk that way about him. I thought you kind of liked the guy."

"Maybe I did. Maybe I changed my mind," Helen said.

Baldo leaned forward. They were arguing about Malfino, he realized.

Jim said, "All of a sudden you're down on the guy. What's the story?"

"He's—he's dangerous, Jim."

Jim laughed heartily. "Dangerous? A guy who works in a church? Listen, Carl's a reformed character. I may be slow-moving, but I'm not dumb. I can see when a man has changed for the better. Like Carl has."

"You really think so, do you?"

"Sure I do!"

Helen uttered a thin, contemptuous chuckle. "Listen to me, Jim. You know the night Carl took me out because it was our anniversary and you couldn't go?"

"Yeah?"

"We went to this night club, him and me. And he hammed it up just like he was my husband. He bought me that flower you saw. It must have cost him five, six bucks. And we had drinks galore at the night club. The check was like around twenty bucks by the time we were through. And I saw his wallet when he paid it. He had a roll you could choke a horse with."

"So?"

"So? Another thing. While we were there, this cop comes over. Off-duty. Carl's on parole and guys on parole aren't supposed to be in places like that. The cop starts putting Carl down. So they get up and go somewhere, and when they come back they're all smiles. It was a payoff. And you know what? Carl sends a bottle of champagne over to the cop's table. Nine bucks for a bottle of champagne, and he sends one with his compliments!"

"What does all this have to do with—"

"Plenty!" Helen cried. "Carl works sweeping out a church. You think they give him ten thousand a year? More like forty bucks a week."

"So?"

"Where does he get the kind of dough he throws around?"

"He's got a rich father."

"I happen to know Carl hasn't had anything to do with his old man in years. The old man threw him out way back. Carl's getting the dough somewhere else. Maybe he's got business contacts. And you know what sort of business."

Jim Keleher said heavily, "You can't work in a church and still be in the rackets. How can you fool the priests?"

"Carl can. Carl could fool the Pope himself!"

"Shut up! Don't talk that way, Helen!"

"Listen, we're getting off the track. I want you to tell him not to come around."

"No," Jim said sullenly.

"Why the hell not?"

"He's my friend."

"Your friend! Your friend! That's all you can say! You big lummox, do you want a crook playing with your kid?"

"All of a sudden you don't trust Carl."

"I'm afraid for Papa. One more bit of trouble and they put him away for the rest of his life. I don't want Carl to get him mixed up in anything."

"Your father can look out for himself. He's as smart as Carl. Smarter. Anyway, he's an old man now."

"Carl can twist him around. Carl can make him do things again. Throw him out of the house, Jim!"

"No."

"Why are you so stubborn?"

"I can't do it. I won't. Helen, I just refuse."

"You're afraid of him."

"Who says?"

"It's because he was caught on that job and you weren't. You feel guilty. You feel like you owe him something. And you're afraid of him because you took his woman away."

"That isn't so," Jim said without conviction.

"Don't you know the Siciliano, Jim Keleher? Oh, sure, sure! You know what the man feels. You're afraid, afraid!"

"Cut it out, Helen!"

"Look, you're sweating! Why don't you throw him out? You're big enough—"

"He's my friend," Jim said guiltily. "Tommy likes him too. And so do you really. I can take care of myself—and will you drop the subject? I got to sleep. It's past midnight."

A pause, then an outburst, "Don't you love me, Jim?"

Tenderly. "Sure I love you. More than the world. Do I have to tell you that?"

"Tell me, tell me, every day, Jim. And show me."

"Darling—"

"Show me!" Frantically. "Now! Right now! God—"

Baldo turned his head aside, hearing things he had no right to hear, but with a queer sense of relief. At least so much was well with his little girl—and there was hope. The bitter quarrel had gone into the flux of love. Harsh breathing now, and the squeak of bedsprings, a woman's small shriek of joy in pain, a deep sigh of pleasure. Tears came, but now blessed tears and the benign love for his child.

For the first time in seventeen years, Baldo fell into a deep sleep of satisfaction and a smile touched his mouth as the night passed.

Toward dawn, however, he awoke with a start. One part of his dreaming mind had been gnawing away—

Helen too was worried about Malfino.

This business about Jim Keleher and that robbery that had sent Carl to prison. What was that about? Jim was not the type to get on the wrong side of the law. Could he have been talked into some job? Maybe to drive a getaway car? Act as lookout? What?

Whatever it was, Carl had kept a shut mouth and taken the fall by himself. That same fall that brought him to Dannemora just before Helen had her baby and had married Jim. Carl and Jim—had they made a deal? A deal about Helen?

Yeah, yeah!

Baldo threw back the covers and sat up, drenched with sweat, feeling the mugginess of the night. Carl had his son-in-law in some grip. And Jim, big, stolid, handsome, hard-working, stupid—in thrall because of guilt. What guilt? He had taken Carl's woman!

And Helen?

She mistrusted Carl—or was it herself? Did Carl still hold some physical attraction that she could not fight? Baldo grimaced with pain. The terror of impotence—helplessness. Was she fighting for—who? Father? Husband? Child? Self?

Jim Keleher came out of the bathroom, razor in hand. "You up, Pop? What about coffee? I feel great!"

Baldo smiled grimly. "Yeah, sure! I'd like coffee, Jim! If only we could keep it like this—"

Later, he glanced into the bedroom. Helen was still asleep, her head thrown back, drugged, snoring softly, her breasts rising and falling slowly and deeply. Her mother had looked like that, Baldo reflected, glancing at the picture on the dresser, on the night Helen had been born. He turned aside and sat by the window.

And finally the path was clear.

Harry Northrup was at his desk early the following morning. He was ostensibly occupied with an East Side homicide case, but it was a simple affair, and the problem that still troubled him was the *Balthazar* and its cocaine.

Midway through the morning, he was visited by Dan Rollins, one of the detectives he had assigned to keep tabs on the *Balthazar* and its crew. Rollins, a chunky, businesslike man with plump pink cheeks and deceptively innocent eyes, was one of the department's most effective men.

He spread his hands noncommittally and said, "I've been talking to the captain of the *Balthazar.*"

Northrup raised an eyebrow. "Sanchez himself?"

"None other. He came ashore last night and I introduced myself to him in a bar. Told him I was a businessman with interests in Venezuela and Mexico." Rollins grinned. "Damned good thing I studied Spanish, you know?"

"Do you think he saw through it?"

"Not a chance," Rollins said with the complacent positiveness that was one of his more annoying characteristics—even though his complacency was invariably well founded. "By the end of the evening we were crying in each other's rum. He's got a wife at home and a mistress he loves dearly in Chile. I told him about a sweetie I have in Caracas."

"You always did have a good imagination," Northrup muttered. "So you're Sanchez' pal. What of it?"

"He's with the revolutionary group."

"Sure of it?"

"Absolutely. He as much as told me so in as many words. He let me have it to understand that when Morales took over, the divorce laws were going to be liberalized and his wife was getting the boot in favor of the Chilean sweetheart."

Northrup leaned forward tensely. "What about the rest of them on board? All Morales men?"

Rollins shook his head. "So far as I could gather, no. The rank and file of the crewmen are loyalists. They simply think this is just another assignment for them—ferrying a bunch of diplomats up to New York. It's my guess that nobody below the very top ranks has any inkling of why that ship is really here. But Sanchez does. By the end of the evening I was kidding him about coca leaves. He offered to mail me a couple when he gets back home."

"Suppose you gave the show away, Dan?"

"Now, would I do a thing like that? Harry, I tell you Sanchez was like a babe in my arms. He told me everything

I wanted to find out, and got nothing out of me. I deserve a bonus, Harry."

"Take it up with the commissioner." Northrup tapped his fingertips on the desk top. "I'm glad we waited, Dan. If we had gone busting onto that ship demanding to see the captain, we'd have tipped our hands right at the start."

"What now?" Rollins asked. "Going to have Washington notify the legitimate government that there's dirty work in New York Harbor?"

"Washington knows," Northrup said. "I can't make any move until that junk comes off that ship."

"What are we waiting for?"

"Scarpa."

Northrup looked up with cold eyes. "Scarpa's the key," he said grimly. "The key to the *Balthazar*. The key to Pereira, I hope."

Rollins bit into a wedge of coffee cake. "Why so?"

Northrup began prowling his office, worrying over a train of thought that had become clear. "Now why would Malfino be so desperate to line up Scarpa?" he demanded, and answered his own question. "It could only be because he needs the old man."

"Needs him for what?"

"Some reason." Northrup stared down at the park below from which the shouts of Chinese children at play could be heard. "I'm not sure. It's got to be connected with Scarpa's daughter. The whole relationship is funny. But I hope that—"

"Yeah?" Rollins waited encouragingly.

Northrup turned. "It must be Scarpa's name. He's done seventeen years at Dannemora. He's just a tired old man who wants to be left alone, but I think that news reached South America. I think Malfino's trading on the old man's reputation."

"Why?"

"Because his own isn't good enough. These Morales people have got to move this stuff into the underworld. Somehow, somewhere, Malfino sold them a bill of goods. They can't move the stuff except into the right channels. They can't get into the right channels without assurance that security is tight all the way. They've got to have a big man—a man with reputation, to make sure they're not being led into a trap."

"Why can't Malfino pick out someone else? Someone who

really counts?" Rollins demanded. He lifted a mug of cold coffee and spat. The coffee was always cold by the time it was delivered from the snack bar on the first floor. "Why Scarpa?"

"Because Scarpa can't take the play away," Northrup argued worriedly. "Baldo's going to be forced to move whether he likes it or not. I hope he moves in my direction. I hope he makes the right decision. I'm worried about that old man."

"You, Mr. Northrup? Sentimental in your old age?"

Northrup opened the door. "Out," he ordered.

The door closed.

Northrup continued to pace the office. It was the waiting, the damned waiting that had gotten under his skin. With an impatient gesture, he picked up the telephone and called a familiar number.

"Free tonight?"

Donna said sweetly. "What's your offer?"

"Dinner. The Leonardo da Vinci."

"Date," said Donna.

It was an enchanting evening, swimming with gin and tonic, and Donna was never more understanding. But an old man's haggard face floated between his thoughts and the surcease of Donna.

12

Friday, mid-afternoon. The weather was hot, with the thermometer at eighty.

Baldo sat in his room, shirtless, studying a newspaper devoted to the racetrack with unseeing eyes. In his time, he had dropped hundreds of thousands without thought. Now a five spot was out of the question. He could not engage his interest in the unfamiliar names of new horseflesh. His grandson was taking an afternoon nap. His daughter was in another room, dressed in a light summer cotton frock, staring at a television screen. The doorbell rang. There was the sound of Helen's footsteps—quick, nervous—and the door opened.

"Jim here?" Carl Malfino asked.

Helen said, "You know he's not."

Baldo opened the door of his room.

Malfino turned a speculative eye. "Hey, Baldo! How's it been? Hot, huh? Let me send over some air conditioning? I got a friend in the business."

Baldo said, "We don't need it. I like it hot."

A bedroom door opened, and a little boy rushed out. "Uncle Carl! Uncle Carl!"

Malfino swung the boy high into the air, up to the ceiling, and the child squealed with delight, smelling plaster and trembling with the ecstasy of fear and the reassurance of the powerful grip of strong hands.

"Put him down!" Helen said strongly.

Malfino calmly swung the boy about like a sack of flour. "Upsy! Downsy!"

"Put him down, damn it!" Helen said strongly.

Baldo said, "Do what she says."

Malfino smiled with white teeth. "Oh, sure!" he agreed equably. He set the boy down.

"Get back to your room," Helen said sharply. "You've got to rest another fifteen minutes."

Malfino intervened. "He had enough rest. I'll take him down to the park. They've got a sprinkler there. He'll have a good time."

"I don't like him in the street," Helen replied. "With all those gangs."

"I'll watch him," Malfino said. "You come, too, Baldo? The sun'll do you good. I'd like to talk. You can keep an eye on the kid."

Baldo considered the matter. "All right."

Tommy ran to the sprinkler the moment they reached the park. Malfino and Baldo found a park bench. They were silent for a long moment before Malfino put an arm along the back of the bench. Baldo moved away uncomfortably.

"How's it going, Baldo?"

"I'm glad to be back."

"Getting restless?"

"Restless?"

"You know what I mean."

"I never know what you mean."

"You interested in some action?"

"I might be."

"I got to be sure."

Baldo closed his eyes and turned his face to the sun. He was so tired, so tired.

After a time he said, "You got some deal for me?"

"What makes you ask?"

"Don't beat around the bush, Carl. You been playing all this time. You come to Dannemora hinting, this, that! So what?"

Malfino turned an estimating eye at the fierce older face, estimating its depths, calculating. "I don't know, Baldo! I don't know how you feel inside any more."

"I feel okay."

"You don't talk okay."

"I'm talking now."

Malfino sat considering a squirrel which came climbing forward, sniffing for peanuts, bannertail aloft. "Yeah, yeah!" he said thoughtfully. "I could use a man with a name."

"Use how?"

"This goes one way?"

"You're talking to Baldo, snotnose!"

Malfino grinned. "Suppose I'm involved in something. You'd be better off not hearing, no? I mean, you don't want to get involved, too. That what you told me at Dannemora."

"That was at Dannemora."

"I'm not talking you into anything?"

Baldo arose with an air of impatience. "Forget it, Carl. I put out some feelers. I got all the propositions I need—"

Malfino rose hastily. "Now wait! It's a shipment of cocaine in a certain place—"

Baldo came back with a jolt. "Junk?"

Malfino shrugged. "What—junk? It ain't real junk. Not like heroin. This stuff is used by kids. What junk?"

"Go on," Baldo said heavily. "If you don't move it, somebody else will. Right?"

"Right!" Malfino said, pleased. "Now let's talk business." The position of the shipment was briefly outlined. "This is a political situation. These people don't know the right people who can handle this stuff—move it in the right places. It's got to go through the mobs, you know that—"

"What mobs?"

Malfino gave a quick, accurate description of a dozen mobs in the larger cities who were prepared to handle large shipments of narcotics. He was acting as a middleman between key handlers and the South Americans. He had the assurances of one hundred thousand dollars of financing for the first shipment. As he went on, his eyes gleamed with ferocious enjoyment at the magnitude of the operation. Baldo brought him up short.

"Wait a second! What's so big? One hundred thou—" For this type of handle, it's ridiculous!"

Malfino shook his head. "Not this first shipment. It's just the beginning. After I pick up the first package, these people can deliver maybe five million dollars in first-class merchandise."

Baldo grimaced. "Tested?"

"I got a top chemist. It's all pure, ready to shoot. But that ain't the end. They use the dough for guns, flamethrowers, grenades, maybe small tanks, things like that. I lined up an Egyptian ready to sell this stuff Russia's been shipping. Frankly, those guys in Egypt are making a good thing of that surplus stuff they're getting for free—"

"Hey! You're going too fast!" Baldo protested. "First junk. Then hardware! On cocaine? The whole country don't take enough for that—"

Malfino made an impatient gesture. "Once they take over this country, they use it for a base. Red China," he added impressively. "I got it from a guy who worked in the U.N. He told me—"

"What guy?"

"He's dead now," Malfino said after a pause. "Anyhow, the real stuff moves through Hong Kong and Shanghai. Right now, the trouble is to get it into this country, because the Far East boats are under suspicion. This way, the stuff can move to a country where it's safe in warehouses. That way we got control of a country. A whole country. You know how many tons of opium come out of Manchuria alone? All moving through Turkey, Egypt, Italy, France, where it's converted—"

Baldo listened with grudging respect to an analysis in depth of an illicit international traffic whose dimensions he had not suspected.

"—And I'm talking heroin!" Malfino concluded, sucking his breath with pleasure. "The real stuff—pure, guaranteed, right into the market at top prices! In two years—"

Baldo grunted sceptically. "You're off in a pipe dream! How do I fit?"

Malfino was brought to earth. "I'll be frank. I need you!"

"Why?"

"You're my convincer with these people," Malfino said briefly. "They never heard of me, and I got to show 'em I got the connections."

"And they heard of Mister Baldo Scarpa?"

"Oh, sure! From here to Buenos Aires! You and Capone! It's your reputation. You can't buy reputation." Scarpa smiled grimly, pleased despite himself, and Malfino went on earnestly to point out that the operation called for Baldo Scarpa to appear as guarantor of the operation.

"Would it work?" Baldo asked sceptically.

"They asked for somebody like Baldo Scarpa! To vouch for me! I told 'em you would."

"They mentioned me by name?" Baldo asked, surprised.

"So help me God."

"Tell me the name!"

"Later."

"Was it Morales?" Baldo demanded.

Malfino grinned. "Give that man sixty-four thousand bucks and a free tube of toothpaste!"

"Juan Morales! After all these years! You say he remembered me? He is in New York?"

"No, not Juan. Two of his sons, Diego and something else. And his brother too."

"Francisco!"

"That's it."

Baldo felt a warm glow. "We had big days together, Juan Morales and I. 1938, it was. And 1939. A long time. But he remembered me?" Baldo asked anxiously. "He asked for me by name?"

"I told you so. I'm not trying to snow you, Baldo."

"All right. So there is cocaine and the Morales family wants me to vouch for you. Is this all?"

"That's all, Baldo. Just come out to Brooklyn and have lunch with me and Diego Morales. Tell him I'm okay, that I can be trusted. Then I give you the money, you hand it to Morales, they give you the C, you hand it to me, and we're set. In business."

"Wait a minute," Baldo said tensely. "*I* hand the money to Morales? *I* bring the junk to you?"

"Well, yes—"

"But that makes me a party to the deal. This goes beyond

vouching, Carl. You want to turn me into a go-between, a courier."

"It'll be worth your while, Baldo. I'll cut you in for ten per cent. That could be anywhere up around a million bucks or more. A million! You know how you could live on a million? Champagne for breakfast!"

"It would look very good, wouldn't it, for me to start living like a millionaire after coming out of prison practically penniless."

"There are ways to cover it up. You could deposit the money in a Swiss bank. No one would know it was yours, and you could draw on it, at least live comfortably for the rest of your life. Then after you're gone Helen and Tommy inherit your money. The police would think it was dough you had stashed away in the old days. Those Swiss banks are tight-lipped. Don't you want to provide for your grandchild, Baldo?"

"And if I am caught?" Baldo asked quietly.

"Caught? Who's to catch? This whole deal will be over quick-quick-quick!"

"You don't think I am being watched by the police? And you? You are on parole. They keep tabs."

"It's dark out on the harbor. All we got to do is get the stuff from the boat to one of the little islands. You bring it to me, I ride it into Jersey, hand it over to someone waiting there. Five or six nights and the whole load is transferred." Malfino's somber eyes were glowing with the excitement of a potential fortune. "I've got this all sewed up, Baldo. I've got a buyer, I've got a seller, all I need is transportation from the boat."

"Which I will not do."

"Look, Baldo—"

"*You* look. They catch me, I get put away forever. The risk is too big. I do not need a million dollars so much as I need my freedom."

"Don't you get it, you're the key to this whole thing! I can get a cash advance to buy the stuff, but the Morales bunch won't sell except to you."

"Use my name if you want to," Baldo said. "And pay me what you want. But I won't mix into this. I won't be a courier for you. Get the stuff from the boat yourself."

"Baldo, Baldo, don't be like that!"

"Do you know what it's like to be a three-time loser? To know how close you are to a lifetime behind bars?"

"Do you know what a million dollars would mean to Tommy? Good clothes. Good school. The finest college. He could be a gentleman, not just come grocer's son."

Baldo rose and faced the younger man somberly. "The answer is no."

Sweat was running profusely down Carl Malfino's handsome face. "All right," he muttered. "All right. Cut my throat, see if I care. You know, I got competition for this C."

"What kind of competition?"

"The other Morales brother's been sniffing around in Harlem. He's got a Spanish gang there interested, people from his own country. Only they've run into some problems trying to finance the deal. Old man Morales specifically said to deal through you, if you were still alive and in circulation. But if you don't come through, well, I might lose the deal altogether. It could even be dangerous."

Baldo closed his eyes again. He got the picture. Rival gangs jockeying for the privilege of picking up this juicy load of cocaine at knockdown prices. And Juan Morales, jumpy and sly as ever, wanting only to deal with someone he knew well. Which meant Baldo. If he lent his name and maybe a little effort, Carl would make the deal and they'd both become rich men.

"I will vouch," Baldo said. "But not take part."

"All right. I won't press it. Maybe after you've talked to Morales you'll decide to help out."

"My mind is made up. I will help you only within the law. They cannot arrest me for vouching for you. But if I actually transport junk, and pass checks back and forth—"

"Tomorrow, then?" Malfino said eagerly. "You can meet me at the church around noon. You know where the church is? Sure you do. I forget, it's your old neighborhood. I'll have Morales there. We'll go out and eat."

Baldo said, "All I do is vouch."

"You don't get ten per cent just for that."

"It's up to you. Get somebody else in the mobs. These people advancing the money."

"I don't trust 'em," Malfino said evenly. "I trust you."

"Why me?"

Malfino's eyes were oddly glazed. "Helen's papa? Tommy's grandpa?" He nodded grimly. "I trust you like I trust myself."

He turned and stamped at the squirrel which darted, startled, and swarmed up a tree. Malfino burst into laughter and walked off.

After a time, Baldo called out, "Come on, Tommy! Let's get home."

Baldo was silent on the way home. So Morales remembered him! He would do business with Baldo Scarpa and only Baldo Scarpa. Merely to say, "I am Baldo Scarpa. I vouch for this man!" It could be a new lease on life.

Helen came out of the kitchen, wiping a hair back. "Where's Carl?"

"He went home."

She sighed. "Good. I don't like him around."

"I thought you liked him," Baldo remarked.

"Did you? I just want him out of here," Helen said vehemently. "I don't trust him."

With good reason, Baldo thought.

"Could we sit in the kitchen and talk over a coffee?" he asked mildly.

"Sure, Papa. I guess so—"

Baldo heaped sugar into the steaming mug, skirting the thought in his mind, while Helen organized dinner, fussing, banging pots, but eventually they were together. She was wearing a sleeveless dress. His eyes were attracted to a vaccination mark on her arm. It was a slender arm—

"Can I talk?" he asked.

"Sure, Papa," she agreed.

"No, not your papa," he protested. "Just an older man. I got no right to talk like your papa. I don't deserve it. Not after all the things I done to you."

"Papa, stop! What's on your mind?" Her eyes were watchful.

He said, "Was there something between you and Carl?"

"We were supposed to get married."

"I mean, did you beat the gun?" he asked bluntly. "Did he take you to bed?"

"Papa! What kind of question is that?" Color mounted to Helen's cheeks. "I don't want to talk about that."

Baldo nodded. "That's an answer," he sighed. "Okay, tell it to the priest, *bambina mia!* I'm just a criminal. How can I talk? Only—" He glanced up grimly. "Tommy is his?"

She made a gesture of pain. "Oh, Papa—"

Baldo touched his daughter's wrist. "Maybe he wants you again? Eh? Maybe he's pestering?"

Helen's voice was low. "I'm married to Jim, Papa. What do you think I am? I don't let Carl touch me."

"But sometimes it's hard?"

"Yes."

Baldo nodded. "You're a woman, *bambina*, and you've been had by this man. He has a hold on you forever through the baby. He touches you and the belly turns to water? Eh?"

She lowered her head. "Sometimes I'm so afraid, Papa. So afraid if he reaches out his hand for me. I think I would go with him. I couldn't help myself."

"Bambina, bambina!"

Baldo hunched his shoulders and walked off to his room. Helen called, "That man called again, Papa."

"Northrup?"

"He wanted to know if you had a job yet."

"I wish he'd mind his own business," Baldo muttered.

"He wanted to know if you'd take lunch with him, Papa. I told him you'd call back if you had anything to tell him."

"I have nothing to tell," Baldo said, closing the door. But it was a lie. He had plenty to tell Northrup now. Harry Northrup! A tough guy with a feather in his hat. He had it all figured out, Baldo thought grimly. He knew that Carl Malfino was up to something that would involve him, and that sooner or later Baldo would be approached. Baldo did not know whether Northrup was aware of what Carl was involved in. But certainly Northrup suspected plenty.

Baldo kicked his shoes off and stretched out on the bed. Up till this afternoon, he could have told the inquisitive Northrup nothing. Now Carl had made his move, and there was much to tell. A few words from Baldo and the police would move in to end all of Carl Malfino's bright dreams of wealth.

But the way of the squealer had never been Baldo Scarpa's way. Let Northrup look out for himself. Baldo had no love for Carl Malfino, but he had none for the district attorney's office either. Let dog eat dog, Baldo thought. It was not his affair. He was an old man, no longer concerned with matters such as this. He had no reason to squeal. Prison had aged him, but it had not changed him quite *that* much.

He smiled. Juan Morales still remembered him! That felt good! Baldo closed his eyes and relaxed.

13

The following morning, shortly after eleven, Baldo left the apartment without telling Helen where he was going, and boarded a train for Brooklyn. Within half an hour he was on Flatbush Avenue. He did not immediately go into the church. He looked around, amazed at how hectic the street had become since his last time here. Shiny new banks and department stores had sprung up. The old trolleys were gone, and brightly painted buses now maneuvered down the crowded street. He went into the church.

In the old days, Baldo Scarpa had been a sporadic church-goer. His wife had been very devout, but Baldo himself had stayed away from church as often as he dared. Now, though, he was grateful for the cool darkness of the church. He slipped into a rear pew and sat with head bowed as though in prayer. Prayer which failed to come.

After what seemed like a long while, a hand touched his shoulder.

"Let's go, Baldo," Carl Malfino murmured.

Baldo followed the younger man out the western door and into the garden. "Where's Morales?" he asked.

"He'll be meeting us outside."

They moved on into the garden. A slim, Latin-featured man in his late twenties or very early thirties came toward them, grinning broadly, holding out a hand.

"*Buenos dias,* Carl!"

"Morning, Diego. I've got someone with me for you to meet. Baldo Scarpa, Diego Morales."

Diego Morales turned to Baldo with glowing eyes and said in formal, stiffly-phrased English, "It is a very great pleasure to meet you, Mr. Scarpa. I have heard so much about you from my father. He has the highest praise for your acumen."

Baldo said, "You don't remember that I met you years ago?"

Diego looked blank. "Indeed?"

"Better than twenty years ago, it was. You were running around in knee-pants then. And your brother practically a baby. You don't remember?"

Laughing, Diego said, "Twenty years is such a long time for a man my age, Mr. Scarpa!"

"Let's go get some food," Malfino interjected. "I've got to be back at work by one."

He led them across the street to a two-story restaurant that fronted on Flatbush Avenue. A table had already been reserved in the dining room. They ordered a round of cocktails. Baldo, in an expansive mood, reminisced about his career in South America. Morales listened, obviously impressed.

Finally he said, "Mr. Malfino has told you of the transaction we wish to make?"

Baldo nodded. "He explained the whole thing."

"My father has the greatest trust in you, Mr. Scarpa. He has never forgotten your services to him in the years gone by. Before we set out, he urged us to find you and put our proposition to you." Diego's smile was unwavering. "Mr. Malfino is a close friend of yours, is he not?"

"He certainly is," Baldo said, bringing a heavy hand on Malfino's knee. "He almost married my daughter."

"Almost?"

"He got sent up for five years," Baldo said jovially. "Meanwhile the girl married a good friend. But Carl is always high with me. Right?"

Malfino laughed uncertainly. "Right."

"Good! We had no doubts," Diego remarked, "but we are instructed to deal only with safe people. Like you."

"Carl is like the family," Baldo said.

"Let's get on," Malfino said impatiently.

"Very well." Diego glanced sharply at Malfino. "We have been in New York too long now. We must get home with the money and equipment. How soon can we—?"

"Next week!" Malfino said quickly. "The pickup is Monday night, unless it's too clear. Let's hope for fog. Then the rest each night until we have it all."

"And payment?"

"As agreed," Malfino said. "Cash, in six equal installments, one with each pickup."

"Very good." Diego rose. "You will excuse me while I telephone my brother?" he said with an air of precision, and left.

Malfino turned to Baldo, mopping his neck with relief. "We've got it made!" He blew out his cheeks and grinned.

"What did you expect?"

"You'd be surprised. Yesterday it was like pulling teeth. It went because you were here. I'm being truthful."

"Maybe they're getting impatient."

"Damn right they're impatient. Well, pretty soon they'll be home and we'll be rich." Malfino put his hand on the older man's heavy shoulder. "Baldo, take the stuff for me. Ten percent."

Baldo shook his head. "No."

"You're not thinking right. It's money—big money, and only the beginning."

"Not junk. I don't carry junk."

"Why be so stubborn? This is a simple operation."

"Then do it yourself."

Malfino beat a fist in exasperation. "I can't, God damn it! I got to be waiting for the getaway in a fast boat. You take an outboard job to bring the junk to me. I'm waiting with a power launch, and I take it around Staten Island and across Jersey to the drop. A two-man operation. I need a man to trust."

"You forget your other people. Let them make the pick-up," Baldo suggested stolidly.

"I can't let 'em know where it's coming from!" Malfino turned with an ugly look. "You, only you, Baldo! Can't you see? It's touch and go enough with Morales. This is a warship, for Christ's sake! How loose can they afford to get with this?"

Baldo shrugged and came back to a glass of wine.

The young South American was grinning cheerfully as he resumed his seat. "My brother is pleased," he announced. "We have messages urging us to return home. Well, now we can act. I have told him we have a definite commitment with you."

"Music to my ears!" Malfino announced. "I was sure Albero's bunch would beat us out. Let's drink! To the partnership—Scarpa and Malfino Distributors! And to the Morales family!"

An hour later the luncheon broke up when Malfino with an exclamation ran back to work at the church. Diego Morales offered Baldo a ride to Manhattan in his hired, chauffeured Rolls.

Baldo settled down gratefully in the plush seat. The car was air-conditioned and moved as though gliding—a far cry from the subway, Baldo thought. They made light conversation, touching not one bit on crime, junk, revolution, or prisons. His Spanish had gone to rust in two decades, but he still knew some phrases. Morales politely fell into English. Baldo got off at Fifth Avenue and Fourteenth Street and walked back to the tumbledown street on which he lived.

It was tempting enough, he reflected. If anything went wrong, the stuff could be dumped in the river. What really could go wrong? But suppose it did? Could Baldo Scarpa be picked up for junk? The headlines—Junk! Baldo Scarpa! He would rather die.

Harry Northrup picked up the telephone. Dom Maestroangeli was calling.

The parole officer said, "Message from Ed Tompkins, Harry. He was on Malfino again this morning—"

"Yes, sure!" Northrup was getting bored.

"Listen! Malfino had lunch with Diego Morales again, across the street from the church."

"So?"

"So something ought to interest you. A third man at the table. Baldo Scarpa."

Northrup sat up. "This straight, Dom?"

Maestroangeli chuckled and described pungently and accurately the luncheon meeting. "They acted like they were celebrating. Like they struck a deal, you know?"

Northrup was silent.

"Maybe," he said cautiously. "It looks promising."

"Promising?" Maestroangeli protested. "Here we break ourselves and you find it promising. What now?"

"Nothing. Just let it ride. And tell Ed not to stumble over Malfino. I've got some things to do."

Northrup slammed the receiver, thought for a moment, then grabbed a hat, and stalked out. "Take messages!" he ordered.

"Yes, Mr. Northrup."

"If Rollins calls in, tell him things might, they just might be starting to move. Got that?"

"Yes, Mr. Northrup."

The sound of a crying baby could be heard. The house had a stale smell of cooking. Garbage pails stood at the landings. Apartment 3-C. The doorbell was out of order and he knocked. After a moment, the door opened and he found himself facing a good-looking somewhat worn woman of thirty.

"Mrs. Keleher?"

The woman looked blank. "Yes?"

Northrup introduced himself. "I wonder if your father is home?"

Helen turned impassively. "Papa?"

A harsh voice answered. "Who is it?"

"Mr. Northrup."

Baldo Scarpa came out in an undershirt and a pair of un-laundered chino pants. Tufts of white hair sprouted from his chest. He was gaunt and lean and there was no welcome in his eyes.

"You come into my home, Mr. Northrup?" he said stiffly.

"You don't come to me, Mr. Scarpa, and I didn't want to send anyone for you."

"Papa—" Helen began impulsively.

Baldo held up a hand. "It's all right, Helen. It's only Mr. Northrup. He's a square shooter."

"Yes, Papa!"

Helen turned and went to the rear of the apartment, impassive and contained, scooping up her little boy on the way. Her manner was the timeless, hopeless manner of the women of the island from which her forebears came. Northrup gazed about the clean little apartment with its devotional pictures on the wall, a sideboard, television, a parakeet trilling, cheap but attractive decorations—

Northrup said, "Just a word, Baldo."

"Please—"

Baldo put on a coat and they went into the hall. Baldo closed the door of the apartment and indicated a place on the stairs. "We won't be disturbed."

Northrup said, "Can I talk in confidence, Baldo?"

Baldo nodded. "In confidence."

"This means a word of honor not to tell anybody?"

"Yes."

"I've been in touch with the governor's office."

Baldo gazed watchfully.

Northrup went on. "Your commutation had a lot of conditions."

"Conditions?" Beads of sweat were starting.

"Oh, sure!" Northrup started a cigar and offered one. Baldo shook his head.

"What conditions?"

"No consorting," Northrup said, "among other things. Baldo, you put yourself on the right side with those medical experiments, but that wiped the slate. It didn't give you a ticket forever. I'm in a position to send you back."

"You couldn't do that!"

"Oh, I could!" Northrup said grimly. "I sure could, for violation of the terms of the commutation—the conditions laid down by the governor."

The trickle of sweat turned into a rivulet that ran into Baldo's collar. "What do you want with me, Mr. Northrup?"

"Cooperation."

"How can I cooperate? With what?"

A child came shouting up the stairs, saw the two men talking, and retreated, wide-eyed and wary, and then dashed into the street calling for her mother. Northrup gazed at his cigar nicely. "You had lunch today with two men in a restaurant in Flatbush Avenue. I'd like to know what that was about."

Baldo said with bitter humor, "Baseball, Mr. Northrup. The weather. And the stock market. I got plans to make a killing in the stock market. I live in this dump because all my money is in stocks and bonds."

"I want a better answer," Northrup said.

Baldo shook his head. "No, Mr. Northrup! You won't send me back to prison just for no lunch. Nothing happened at that lunch except three men having a good time. Nothing criminal. Nothing to destroy a man's life. I could be sent back—but not by you. Not on those facts."

Northrup threw away a cold cigar.

"All right, Baldo. One hand washes the other. You help me and I'll help you."

"Help me? How?"

"Give me Malfino! Before he does something to your family."

"What should he do to my family?" Baldo asked stolidly. "I can protect my family. I got a son-in-law. I don't need help."

Northrup rose, "Baldo, I'll put it on this level. I'll give you a week to make up your mind whose side you're on. By talking to you, I'm exposing my hand. I know you can go back and talk to Malfino—but I put you under a word of honor. I'm trusting you to do the right thing. Will you mention any of this to Malfino?"

Baldo rose. "No, Mr. Northrup. But I promise nothing."

"I'm trusting you, Baldo," Northrup said. "Make up your mind whose side you're on."

I tried, he thought. *I tried and it didn't work.*

He nodded curtly and left, shaking his head. On the curb, standing in the hot sun, watching the busy street, he noticed with vagrant curiosity a large sedan pick its way past pushcarts and baby carriages. Its occupants were Puerto Rican, he thought, and then his mind went back to the gaunt old man staring into the street from behind a curtained window. Northrup shook his head.

Criminals! No sense! No sense at all!

14

By evening some of the heat had ebbed. Jim Keleher had not returned for dinner. Tommy was restless and had asked to play before bedtime. Baldo agreed to take the child to play in the street.

"What did Mr. Northrup want?" Helen demanded.

"Nothing, nothing!" Baldo replied angrily. "Just a routine business. The guys are like that. I'll tell you later, maybe."

"Now!"

"No, later! I got to think."

The old man sat on a wooden chair in front of the house, while the boy amused himself with a plastic hoop. The sun was beginning to go down now. Baldo watched the boy, taking pride in his long legs, in his precocious agility.

He thought about the events of the day. No one wanted to let him be. Carl Malfino, urging him to become a carrier of cocaine. And Northrup, begging him to turn informer. Couldn't they understand that he wanted none of them? That he just wanted to live out his days in quiet?

"Don't go near the curb, Tommy," he called. "You'll get hit by a car."

"I'll be careful, Grandpa!"

Baldo nodded without relaxing his vigil. The boy had grown to like him, since that first rebuff at Grand Central Station.

Tommy had been afraid of the gaunt old man, but the fear had worn off. They were good friends now. Baldo Scarpa! To end his days as a playmate for a five-year-old. But he made no apologies. His big days were behind him. This was what he wanted now.

"Look!" Tommy cried. "Here comes Uncle Carl!"

"Where?"

The boy pointed. Baldo leaned forward and saw Malfino coming up the block, striding jauntily along. Baldo's stomach went tense. Why did Malfino have to haunt this street so much? Why couldn't he stay in Brooklyn?

"Getting the last drop of sunshine, huh?" Malfino asked as he came up. He tossed Tommy into the air, caught him, set him down. "How's it going, Baldo?"

"You'd think you didn't see me all day."

"Not for five hours." Malfino stared suspiciously, then let his face clear. "I finished up early at the church. The church," he grinned, laughing. "I came to bring Tommy something." He produced a small package and handed it to the boy, who unwrapped it with eager hands. It was a brightly painted mechanical top with a deep hum. Malfino wound a key and set it down. Tommy gazed seriously, rapt, as it hummed and danced to a wobbling end.

Baldo said glumly, "What do you say?"

The boy looked up. "Thanks, Uncle Carl."

Malfino smiled. He was always bringing toys for Tommy. Why? Was this preparation for the day? The day when Tommy would have to look to a new father? Carl Malfino was playing a subtle, patient game, Baldo Scarpa thought vengefully, but when the game was up—when he no longer needed Baldo Scarpa's help, what would happen to the little family? He stared into the dark features of his grandson, laughing with pleasure into those of Carl Malfino—

Eh! Eh, the boy was also a Scarpa. Baldo's blood ran through Helen and through the boy—

And then Malfino was talking in a low voice. "All set, Baldo. Monday night. Weather bureau claims a chance of fog the next few days. Maybe till Wednesday. We can make three trips."

"I want no part of junk!" Baldo said stubbornly, but less convincing in his own ears.

Malfino's hand reached out cruelly and took Baldo Scarpa's

and pressed. The two men were locked in a clash of wills. Neither would glance aside.

Malfino's voice held an edge. "What's the matter, Baldo? You need some time? Okay! But I'm beginning to think maybe you're just an old fart!"

How long can I keep it up? Scarpa wondered desperately. *The bones can crack and I won't give in!* But would he be able to keep the tears of weakness from his eyes?

"I do nothing without respect, Malfino," he said, clenching his mouth. "Remember! Respect!" An eternity of pain passed.

Disgruntled, Malfino dropped the old man's hand. "Okay," he said, rubbing his knuckles. "I give you respect! I also give you one day to make up your mind. Tommy's granpapa, I give respect."

He turned aside and smiled at the child whose attention had been attracted. "Just a game, Tommy," Malfino advised, forcing a smile. "Just a game."

Baldo turned aside, wringing his hand, wondering at the delay in coming to a decision. It would be easy to get rid of this Malfino! he thought. One word to the man in the district attorney's office and Malfino would go away for a long time. Was that what it came to? Was that the way open to Scarpa? Or a gun—

Malfino was saying, "Baldo, I give you one more chance—"

A sedan made a turn in the street and came to a halt in front of the curb, double-parked. Baldo noticed the occupants without interest. Five or six men. Latin types, they seemed. Puerto Ricans. But well dressed, better than most Baldo had seen. Four of them were out of the park, looking around for an address.

Then there was pointing, shouting—

"*Allá Malfino—*"

"*Y Scarpa!*"

"*Matamos!*"

Baldo was on his feet when the guns appeared.

"The cellar!" Malfino cried. Like a cat he had dropped, whirled, rolled about, fallen into the passageway that led to the courtyard of the tenement. Baldo was down, panting, covering up, cowering— And then the face of Malfino, returning, and a hand out for Tommy, and retreat into the passageway. A rattle of bullets, quick, a burst, silence, a rattle, then a screeching car. Baldo ran, not looking back, until he was deep in the cellar of the house, near the

furnace. He found himself, panting and dizzy, in a black
space smelling of coal and dust. A distant sound of shots,
widely spaced—a blowing of whistles and after an age the
scream of police sirens. And then a curious silence. The
gasping breath was his own, the loud hammering was his
heart—

"Oh, Jesus, Oh, Jesus—" his voice was saying. "Tommy!
Where Tommy—?

After a time, ages it seemed, through a nightmare non-
time, non-space, he groped his way toward a patch of day-
light.

PART THREE

15

They sat in the squad room, impassive, containing their grief, showing to the world a timeless response to the probe of the law. Authority sat behind the partition. Strong, bulky men wearing guns came and went. Typewriters were clacking and occasionally low voices were in conversation with men elsewhere.

"Eh, bambina," Baldo muttered, groping for his daughter's hand.

"No, Papa." The hand was silently withdrawn.

Jim Keleher clasped and unclasped his great hands in an agony of grief. "The little boy," he kept repeating. "So tiny. So small. Why did he have to die?"

There was no answer.

Keleher turned to the stricken old man. "I don't get it," he said wonderingly. "You, Pop? Why would anyone shoot at you? What was it about?"

Baldo Scarpa raised a head and the ligaments of his throat were like strings. "The old days," he muttered evasively. "A lot of people gave me the black mark."

"What black mark?"

Keleher arose and paced from watercooler to the window covered with steel mesh. He stared at the rising moon, and turned, puzzled and frowning, quelling the pain within a bursting heart. "You get the black mark," he said thickly. "But it's the little boy who got killed."

Baldo shrugged in wordless grief.

Keleher said, "You lift those shoulders. What does that mean?"

A thick-set detective looked up from a typewriter and

commanded quiet. Keleher nodded, letting the fat muscles of his jaw work convulsively. He came back to his wife.

"You know anything?" he demanded. "Anything you ain't telling me? I can't stand to see you like this."

Helen shook her head. "Sit down," she said coldly. "You're making a show."

He paused, summoning strength to control the pain. "Why don't you cry?" he begged. "Why in hell don't you cry?"

"Isn't it too late?"

Keleher paused, stupid and hurt. "Too late?"

"I begged you to do something," she said in a flat voice. "I wanted you to get rid of Carl."

Keleher sat, taken aback by her strange indifference.

"My baby's dead," she said bitterly. "Men with guns killed my baby. How would crying help my baby? I needed a man for that. You're no man."

One surge of pain after another.

Keleher paused uncertainly, struggling to grasp his wife's meaning. "I was at work." His voice choked. "If I was there, I'd have torn 'em apart, but I was running the store. Can't you please see that?" He was pleading for understanding.

Helen shrugged.

"Yeah, sure," she agreed, cruel and indifferent. "You were running the store."

Keleher rose and grasped the steel mesh of the window and stared at a black sky.

"God help me!" he prayed. "God help me!"

Dan Schreiber came out, escorting the last of the neighbors. John Costas. A tailor, whose quick glance told the situation behind the partition. He had seen nothing, heard nothing, knew nothing. Oh, sure! Bullets, but he had been looking in his lunch basket and when he had looked up, it was all over. Variations on a familiar theme.

"Keleher!"

Jim Keleher arose nervously and went behind the partition. His last glance at his wife was pleading.

"Bambina," said Baldo in a low voice.

"Yeah, Papa?"

"My fault. Not Jim's."

Helen lit a cigarette. "I'm not blaming you, Papa! You're an old man. When we get home, I'll make you soup."

"Soup?"

"Papa! You got spots on your suit. Let me fix you."
Helen took a handkerchief, dabbed it with spit, and rubbed
specks of coal dust from his coat. Her quick, competent dabs
covered his face, coat, hands, fly. *I'm a child*, he thought
bitterly. *She touches me there like it don't count.*

"Please!" he said, embarrassed.

"Oh, sure," she replied indifferently. "I just want you to
look nice for these people."

Keleher came out soon enough, rubbing his mouth uncertainly, followed by the detective, Dan Schreiber. He came
forward and planted himself before the others.

"Honey—"

Helen looked up, showing a white mask of indifference.
"Yeah?"

"I can hang around and take you home," Jim Keleher
said, "or I can get back to the store. I got an hour's work
to close up, and then I can call for you."

"I don't need you," Helen said.

"Oh, Jesus!"

Jim Keleher waited, torn. "We got a wake, and a funeral
after the autopsy—"

"Autopsy?" Helen asked. "They'll cut my baby?"

Schreiber kneeled gently. "It's the law, Mrs. Keleher,"
he explained. "It won't show. The baby will look just like
an angel. Take my word."

Helen shrugged. "It don't matter. I was only asking."

Keleher said, "I'll be back. I can't figure out what the
hell's the matter with her? I was at the store, working. How is
it my fault? Pop, you tell her—" Heart bursting, he strode
out of the station house into a warm drizzle and found his
way to the warehouse where he sat in darkness, held on a
leash by the hate in his wife's indifference.

Schreiber said, "Mrs. Keleher?"

Baldo Scarpa waited as his daughter rose and glanced
around with an expression of scorn and walked behind the
partition. A humming sound was coming from somewhere—
a fan? Machinery? He could not be sure. A recollection of
the passageway from the cellar was in his mind—and
Malfino, holding a dead child. Malfino, for once guilty! The
scene would remain in mind till death.

"Dead?" Baldo had asked.

Malfino nodded. "He won't need a doctor."

"Who were they?"

"Albero's mob!"

"Albero's? Why would they come for you?"

Malfino was staring off, shaken. "Pereira!" he muttered.

"Who?"

"Pereira! He was theirs."

"What Pereira?"

Malfino's gaze turned back speculatively. "that U.N. guy," he said finally. "Trying to take this play away. You understand?"

Baldo stared into the deadly black eyes of the younger man. The elliptical speech put Malfino into his hands. It also put him into Malfino's. He shivered.

"Did you know they would come?" he asked finally.

"I've been stalling 'em. They wouldn't wait. I gave them the final word. They were out." Malfino listened to the street noises. "Cops outside. I can't be found, or this operation is dead."

Baldo nodded. "I'll take the little boy."

"You won't talk?"

Baldo smiled grimly, nursing a secret thought "No, Carl. This is one deal has got to go through." He tapped his breast with assurance. "I am a man! Baldo Scarpa!" Then the baby was in his arms, white, bloody, surprised in a moment of laughter, cut down— It was clutched in his arms when the police came gingerly down the stairway with ready guns. He was singing an old world song his mother once had sung to him. A lullaby. It was a song he had completely forgotten over the years.

"Baldo! Baldo, are you hearing me?"

He opened his eyes and looked into the square, solid face of Harry Northrup. "What happened?" he whispered.

"You just fell asleep," Northrup said.

"The daughter?"

"Sent her home in the squad car," Northrup said. "Come in. I need a word."

The curious eyes of men were on him when he went behind the partition and took a seat across the desk from the prosecutor. A man with a stenotype machine was seated to his side. Large men were seated about him—Schreiber, Rollins, one with a Dutch name, others. A conventional warning was given.

Northrup said, "Who were they, Baldo?"

"Never saw them before."

"Is that the real truth?"

"The real truth," Baldo said stolidly.

Northrup smoked savagely, chewing the cigar to shreds. "Baldo, I could send you back."

"I know. You won't."

"Why shouldn't I?"

"You know it would be wrong."

"I don't know a frigging thing!" Northrup growled. "You've been playing this game for fifty years. All your life, this closed mouth when the law comes! Okay, but this was a baby they killed. Your daughter's baby. Why did they come after you?"

"I don't know."

"Who could it be who had anything against you?"

Baldo shrugged, and a remembered ghost of a smile tugged at his mouth. "Maybe Nick Spallaccio," he suggested quietly. "Eh?"

Northrup waved a hand of disgust. "Baldo, you stink, for my money. I had some regard for you as a human being. Now I think you're lower than a flea on a dead whore! Baldo!" Northrup pointed a blunt finger. "I've got a witness who says Malfino was with you."

Scarpa held his gaze steady. "Just me and the baby, Mr. Northrup. I think it was all a mistake. These men thought I was somebody else. I can't even give the sizes."

"Were they Spanish?"

"Maybe."

"Irish?"

"Could be."

"Chinese?"

Baldo Scarpa said reproachfully, "Please, Mr. Northrup. This is a serious business."

"You won't tell me a thing?"

"I have told you a lot. Men, an automobile, they were shooting, and I ran with the baby."

Northrup rose and glared with exasperation and threw up his arms. "Criminals!" he growled. "Thick as they come! Their own enemies! I've got more respect for pickpockets than for degraded old men! Take this old bum out of my sight!" Baldo Scarpa arose in frozen silence, venomous hate glinting in his deep eyes, and Northrup laughed harshly and waved his aides out of the smelly alcove.

"Sit down, Baldo!" he said placatingly, and snarled. "Oh,

sit down! I want to figure what to do with you. Take a cigar?"

Baldo said evenly, "I am thinking of the dead."

"Yes, sure!"

Northrup bit off a fresh cigar. "We're alone, Baldo, and
I promise this won't be used by me. It won't go any further.
I made two passes at you, trying to get you to help me. I've
been hinting about Malfino. Frankly, that wasn't a good idea,
but I wanted your help.

"Now, I'm giving you a warning. Sooner or later, Malfino
will destroy your family. Why? Don't ask me why! The guy's
a psychopathic nut! The fact is, he's got a reason. You
don't know the reason, but I do."

Baldo stared into Northrup's hard eyes.

"Reason?" he asked harshly.

"Yes!"

Northrup put aside a yellow form covered with the names
of witnesses. Names, addresses, nothing more. He made a
slow, prolonged ceremony of the cigar before he came to
the point.

"You knew Malfino in Dannemora?"

"Vaguely—"

"He was there on armed robbery, on which he took a
plea?"

"Yes."

"It was a lithography outfit, downtown Manhattan. Payroll
job. Three people were in on it?"

"Three people?"

"Two men and a girl." Northrup let the thought sink in.
"The girl had no idea what would happen. She was just
along for the ride, looking down from a Chinese restaurant,
when the job was pulled."

"What was she doing there?" Baldo asked harshly.

"Lookout."

"Who could make her a lookout?"

"The same one whose still got a hold on her."

Baldo's gaze was fierce and unwavering. "I think you're
a liar, Mr. Northrup."

Northrup accepted the insult. "I wouldn't say she was
technically a lookout. She didn't know what these men were
going to pull. But she thought she was involved, and she
went to the priest, who sent her on to the police."

Baldo stared in a trance. "This girl squealed?"

Northrup smiled grimly. "Baldo Scarpa's daughter? Ridiculous! No, the police just heard her side, and went smelling in the neighborhood. They picked up the two men. One held out—"

"Who?"

"His name was Malfino. The other came through."

"The Irish?"

"The Irish!"

"Jim Keleher?" Baldo whispered wonderingly.

"Let me put it this way. It's in his favor." Northrup blew a plume of smoke at the ceiling. "Keleher would have his tongue cut out first, but he was persuaded it was to save the girl. He went along. He wasn't named in the indictment."

Baldo sat gnawing his hand, seeking to grasp this information through the fog. "But why? Why?" he demanded thickly. "A man has got to be a man. He has got to stand up —even if they tear out the heart. You tell me now the baby's papa is a rat?"

"Who said he was the papa?" Northrup asked cruelly. "Do you think that baby has one drop of Irish? That skin? Those black eyes?"

Baldo swung his head like a goaded animal. "No, no," he panted. "I know this—"

Northrup said harshly. "Sure you do! Malfino screwed the belly off that girl of yours, and you know it! I'll tell you this. In my opinion, just looking at her, she couldn't stand him while it was happening, or after! It was the one and only time. She was afraid of him. Always! From the beginning—"

Baldo stared through a reddish haze. "How could he get into her? How?"

"God knows!" Northrup said.

The two men exchanged glances. A vision was between them—Helen Scarpa, a slender, lovely girl, dark of eye, vibrant with life, naked on the sheets, groaning under the cruel weight of a powerful man with questing, voracious crimson lips—

Northrup interrupted. "When Malfino got sent up, she felt relieved, and good." He continued to smoke.

"And the Irish?" Baldo whispered.

"Somebody had to marry the girl. Who? Who could help? Where could she turn? Mama dead, and papa in the can for life? A lovely girl like that? Keleher, a big, dumb ox, too stupid to handle Malfino, dying to marry her. The Irish don't look for blood on the sheets, but he knew! He knew, and he didn't care. Why should he? Where else would he rate a woman like that?"

"Eh! Yeah, yeah!" Baldo muttered.

"I'll tell you another thing," Northrup added. "I think he did it for Malfino."

"You're crazy!"

Northrup shook his head. "No! Malfino had had Keleher in his hand like this." He made a graphic gesture. "Jim Keleher testified before the grand jury. He let Malfino know. Of course, he claimed it was beaten out of him, and Malfino swallowed that. Or pretended to."

"But why?"

"To cover up for your girl!" Northrup said grimly. "How safe would she be with Malfino if he knew?"

Baldo sat at the desk, feeling the beating of a vein inside a throbbing skull.

Northrup supplied the thought. "On the record, Jim Keleher is the rat. In Carl Malfino's eyes, he squealed. And in his eyes, he's got his friend's woman. What do you say?"

Baldo said painfully, "Still not enough!" he muttered. "Not matter what, it ain't enough."

Northrup arose and grasped the chair. "I'll give you more," he said strongly. "Suppose we held Helen for a material witness? That baby would have been born in the prison ward at Bellevue Hospital. That's what broke that Irish back," he added viciously. "We gave Malfino a lesser plea. He did time while Keleher went back to the grocery business. The only thing—" he paused doubtfully to study the shredded cigar.

"How much does Malfino really know?" he murmured, almost to himself. "He knew Keleher! Too stupid for his own good. Could anybody beat a confession out of that big ox? He could put his hand in the fire and laugh— no nerves, no sense, no feeling! Cut off his balls and he wouldn't talk. Did Malfino really swallow that version? That the cops beat that confession out of him? Is that possible, Baldo?"

A telephone rang shrilly in the squad room. An intolerable moment passed.

"Jim Keleher should not have talked," Baldo Scarpa muttered. "Better to die. Better anything. Can I go?"

"Oh, sure."

The old man arose.

"I am disgraced," he said dully. "I am a tool. I am exposed before the world."

Northrup made a last attempt. "Baldo? You talked with Malfino in the park? Did he say anything to you about a man named Carlos Pereira? From this South American country?" A cold stare greeted him. He shrugged hopelessly. "Malfino means death, Baldo! He'll kill, or be killed! We can't watch him forever. I'd send him back now, if I could, but I've got to play this thing out—"

Baldo turned about. "I am disgraced!" he shouted to the room of men. "I will know what to do! Baldo Scarpa! Baldo Scarpa! Eh? Eh?

He was still shouting as he left the precinct house and walked, hatless, staring, through the warm drizzle along deserted streets that echoed back his name. A name, he thought, that was less than dung.

16

The wake passed, prayers were said, a cortege formed in the street according to ancient custom, and a small, meager group walked along with the small box. For once Malfino was missing while clods of earth were thrown and words in an ancient tongue were uttered. Some eyes wept, but these were not those of the parents—and the old man's eyes were rheumy and weak with grief.

Helen raised a veil. "You going to the store?"

"Not if you want me home," Jim Keleher replied.

"Not especially," she said.

"Honey!" The big man stood in misery. "I wasn't there—"

"I know," she agreed. "You were at the store."

"Is that what I'll hear for the rest of my life?"

"I don't know!" Helen turned about and found the hired limousine and looked at the crowded stones, heaped together, waiting for eternity to pass. "For me, life has passed already."

"Pop?" Jim Keleher pleaded. "What can I do?"

"Get drunk!" Baldo Scarpa advised. "And wait for it to pass." Somewhat apart a sedan was waiting. If he saw the watchful eyes of Harry Northrup, it was not apparent.

It was the afternoon a week later. Baldo Scarpa awoke with a splitting headache and a sour stomach. He rubbed the stubble of his cheeks and flopped back on hot blankets, stuporous with bad whiskey. How long had he been lying there?

The soreness in his breast reminded him of missing laughter and a bright face at the door. The purpose of leaving prison was nothing. The long years in the can nothing. The risk of cancer in his belly gone. For what?

Nothing.

Nothing any more.

He stared at the flaking paint on the wall. The years pressed in on him.

Quiet. Was he alone? Did they care whether he lived or died, now that the child was dead?

Voices were coming from the next room.

"Why? Tell me why?"

"Who knows why? It just happened."

"Deny it!"

"Why deny it? Malfino came here and it happened."

"For my sake. Tell me it's a lie. Do you have to make me suffer?"

"It isn't a lie."

"Honey!"

"It's no lie." The faucet was turned, water splashed into a glass, and the woman's indifferent voice went on. "He wanted me and I accommodated. It's not important."

Baldo shook a stab of horror from his mind. What was all this? This horror?

Jim Keleher said slowly, in grief. "The woman says she saw you through the window! Right here in this room. Didn't you pull down the shade?"

"Maybe not. I don't know. Why?"

"Oh, Jesus! Jesus!" It was a low, animal moan of pain. Baldo rose in fear. *Bambina, no!* he thought. *Not to the husband like that! No man can listen to that!* He paused, and sank back. Did he have the right?

"Why? Honey, why?"

Indifference turned to cruelty. "Why? Why, you weakling?" The voice now was shrill, hateful. "To find out, are you a man! To let the world know, are you a man! Malfino had me—out in the open! Children were watching! What does a man do?"

"I don't know—" The deep voice was bewildered. "I don't get this whole thing—"

Helen shouted suddenly obscenities. Italian, English, gutter filth, picked up out of childhood, the dirt of the world pouring from her mouth.

"Baby killer!" she yelled. "You killed my baby!"

"I can't go against Carl—"

"No man!" she screamed. "No man!" She rushed to the window, then, out to the world. "No man! Let the people know. I was had! Had—and this no man stands, and he wonders! Why? Why?" She rushed back and the ripping sound was a torn dress and her jeer was a paean of hate. "Come on! Get it up! Prove you're a man! Let the people see!"

"Oh, Christ, no!"

Baldo half-opened the door and peered out. Dumb bewilderment and grief were in the square features, the giant frame of his son-in-law. Helen was almost naked, her dress was hanging in shreds, her heavy breasts jouncing with dark aureolas as her wrists slowly were forced apart by her husband's immense strength. The two were staring at each other—Jim Keleher's face stricken with grief, contorted with tears, Helen's mouth was a square measure of hate, like an ancient painting of the Furies. Fully, deliberately, thrusting her breasts forward, she spat. Baldo looked aside in shame.

"Why didn't you get rid of Malfino?" she screamed. "Why didn't you kill him when it was time? What is the hold on you?" Her eyes blazed open. "I had the feeling! I told you he would bring a terrible thing to us! He brought the bullet that killed my baby! Oh, my baby, my baby, my baby!" Suddenly she collapsed on the flooring, moaning in grief, long delayed tears flooding and soaking her nakedness. She looked up with glaring hate. "Fag!"

"Oh, Jesus! She's out of her mind," Jim muttered helplessly. Suddenly, he stood away, dropping her wrists, breathing stertorously, staring at his wife's nakedness. "I can't go against Carl," he muttered. "Not after what I done to him—"

"What? What?" she shouted. "I sent him up! Me! Not you! What is this monkey on your back?"

"He thinks I did," Jim Keleher muttered helplessly. "It's the same thing. If you want him, what can I do? You were his all the time. I knew that when I married. It was understood—"

Her face went pitiful. "Why? Why understood?"

"He had you first. You were his. I only came in because of the baby. I had no right—"

Helen stared with comprehension at something never before said between them. "Oh, my God!" she muttered. "And every time you had me, you were only a stand-in?"

The giant head lowered. "I wanted you from the first day we met. But you were his. Not mine."

"Yes, yes! I see now!" Helen sat helplessly, asprawl, grotesque. "All this time I waited for you to get rid of the man, he was into me through you. Get out!"

"Honey—"

"Get out! Get out! Get out!"

The door slammed, and the floodgates of grief opened. Baldo came out slowly and his daughter's nakedness was like a child's. He found a sheet and put it about her and found the strength to lift her to the sofa. Helpless tears were streaming from her unseeing eyes. He sat beside her and after a time the room was blessed with the dark.

Baldo said, "A cool drink?"

Helen nodded indifferently, dully, staring. "If you like, Papa. Some lemons in the icebox."

He made lemonade and insisted that she drink and she obeyed as she had as a small girl.

"You know?" she said finally, as much statement as question.

"I know," he said.

"What should I do?" she asked.

He touched her hand gently. "Jim is your husband."

"My husband," she muttered. "After what I said? He ought to kill me. After what I did with Malfino!"

"Eh, eh! Don't talk about killing. It ain't always so easy. It's got to be inside. It's no test."

Helen turned. "You would know, Papa?"

He nodded. "I would know. I look back. I don't see what it proves. This is a terrible thing to say."

She smiled wanly, and he felt hope, and then her face clouded. "How can this be explained?"

"How?"

"Malfino touches me and I am water. I have nothing inside that says no. I am so afraid of—what I can do for him. He makes an animal of me. But I'm a woman. It's natural. It's the way men can affect me—but poor Jim! I called him a terrible thing."

He touched her soothingly.

"No, no! Jim is a man. A real man, but gentle, good, it's not in him to kill, and Malfino is a devil. A man who controls through a strange power. A man like Jim cannot be expected to handle a man like Malfino. It takes another kind of man."

Helen turned over in the dark. Her eyes were huge and rimmed with red, her face was haggard but quiet now. To his eyes, in the dusk, she was her mother, and his heart ached for both. "I could take care of this Malfino," he said.

She said, "No, Papa! It's past your time."

"Eh!"

It was a sound. It meant nothing, and then her instinct stirred and she arose and made a dinner—soup, pasta, a bit of cold fish, and they sat in the small kitchen, sipping cold lemonade and talking about family matters. He told her about his childhood and named uncles and aunts and cousins, alive and dead, in the old world, in the new, and with a start, he realized that this was indeed the talk of funerals, of the dead, of the end of a measure of one's life.

"Have children," he said.

"How, Papa?"

"You and Jim," he said. "It will come."

"What should I call this baby?"

"Tommy." He added bleakly, "Maybe—Vincent—James. Even Baldo? Eh?"

In the end they lay in their separate rooms in the empty apartment the miasma that had enveloped this family. Carl Malfino had settled like an evil genius—using Jim's guilt to dominate. He had taken Helen in her moment of grief— as he had known he could. For that alone he should die.

Baldo lay in the dark and considered what was within himself.

17

Churchbells were tolling overhead for noon as Baldo Scarpa entered the church, genuflected, and took a pew. In the dimness, the glint of memorial candles flickering aroused memories of another chapel in the church of St. Dismas, patron saint of thieves, in the big prison at Dannemora. He shivered, and must have slept for suddenly he was aware that Malfino was seated beside him.

"Right on time, Baldo?" Malfino said quietly.

"On a job that's important. You got the money?"

"Not here."

After a moment, Malfino arose and went out to the churchyard where presently he was joined by the older man.

"How's Helen?" Malfino asked politely.

"Eh?"

Baldo shrugged. They were seated on a weathered marble bench not far from iron scrollwork gates. Early roses were in bloom, giving the yard a sweet smell. It was a sunny moment of peace. A complex operation was outlined.

"The dough?" Baldo asked.

"Here."

Baldo studied the check with its stamp of certification. A check in six figures that brought into focus a sense of imminence—a moment delayed, and a door on giant hinges quietly closed. A check between two Latin America trading corporations through a bank in Zurich.

Baldo looked up. "These people take checks?"

Malfino shook his head.

"If you give me the nod, this check will be cashed by safe people right here in New York." He named a quiet, expensive and luxurious hotel facing Central Park South, much frequented by visiting celebrities and Hollywood literary agents and actors. A green and white flag hung before the hotel. "It will be flown to Zurich. When it clears, which will be inside one day, we make the second pass. Okay?"

"Eh! Jets," Baldo said, marvelling.

Malfino returned the check, looking pleased and smug. Quickly, tersely, drawing in the soft loam with a twig, he outlined a procedure that called for two small boats and a split second schedule. "You come to the Jersey side. I'll be tied up near the B. & O. Railway Terminal out in the water. You make the pass and head back to the boat basin. The package has a weight. If you're stopped, over it goes into deep water. Understood?"

Baldo looked thoughtful. "I could dump it," he suggested. "I could change my mind."

The reddish feral look glinted in the depths of the younger man's eyes.

"I would think of my family," he said evenly. "Do I have the nod?"

Baldo looked up somberly. "You got the nod," he agreed. "One condition!"

"Yeah?"

"I'm an old man. Anything happens to me, the daughter gets the dough?"

Malfino's laugh was unpleasant.

"Sure! Why not?" he said lightly. "I revere Helen. I've got her on a pedestal. After all, I was once engaged to her —Papa!" He came back to the plan, arranged for a meeting for money to pass, and suddenly at the sight of a black frock, he turned hastily to the rose bushes and explained that a new variety had been developed in the garden of the church.

The ride back to Manhattan was a haze of fear. But Baldo did not go home. Instead, he wandered around crowded streets, trying desperately to think—pressing against weights on his mind. Off Delancey Street, gazing at a crowd of pushcart peddlers, yelling their wares to swarms of women, he came to a decision. Turning, he walked the distance to Broome Street where a flight of steps brought him down to a restaurant. Checkered red and white cloth covered the tables and there was a smell of clam sauce and pasta in the air.

Four whiskies later he made a telephone call.

"Yes, Baldo?" said a familiar voice. "Where are you?"

"Never mind where I am," he replied thickly. "I'm drunk, so I can tell you something."

"Tell me what?"

Baldo waited, moving a leaden tongue that refused the words of betrayal he had resolved to utter.

The hard voice rose in impatience. "Tell me what? You all right, Baldo?"

"This is hard, Mr. Northrup."

"What's hard?"

"Just one second—"

Baldo steadied himself against the wall of the booth.

"—boat basin," he was saying. "I think, when you get him, you got the man who killed Pereira."

Another man's voice, it seemed, was speaking, not his own.

"—louder, Baldo. Bad connection—"

"From 79th Street. Tonight—"

"Stay there, Baldo! Baldo!—"

The old man stood back, the hearing piece was dangling on its cord, tinnily demanding, demanding— He walked out of the booth—

"Hey!"

Baldo looked at the cashier with unseeing eyes. He went out and walked in the sun, a gaunt old man. He had said what he could. Let the man in the district attorney's office go as far as he could.

Baldo Scarpa!

A familiar door opened and it was Helen. Her eyes looked red but the weeping, he saw, had come from a relieved heart. The house was now cool and orderly and food was on the table—fruit and cakes and wine for company. It was again a decent house, he saw. He sank into a chair and covered his eyes and felt that his shoes were removed by gentle hands.

"Where did you go today, Papa?" Helen asked.

"I saw Malfino," he replied.

"Oh, Papa!"

He caressed her hair and marvelled at its lightness. He smiled wanly. "He won't pester again," he promised. "You have my word."

"I'm not afraid," she replied. "Not any more."

He stared into her eyes. "The truth! I see it is the truth! This thing is burned out of you?"

She nodded.

"It was just twice," she said simply. "The once, when I was a girl—and the other, when I had to get at Jim. I did a terrible thing. Because my baby died."

"It will pass."

"Papa," she said, holding his hand to her cheek. "I have come through hell. A woman can take away from a man and turn him. Whatever happened to Jim, it was my fault. He would come to me like a man, and I was ice, and the heart would go out of him. If he comes back, I will be a woman and he will be a man again."

"Eh, sure!"

He nodded and fell asleep and visions passed of his youth and when he opened his eyes it was dusk.

Keleher opened the door and looked into the darkened flat. The child's room was empty, but dishes had been cleaned and stacked. The house had been dusted. It was tidy.

"Helen?"

And she was at the door of the bedroom, wiping swollen and bloodshot eyes.

"Jim?"

He strode into the living room and filled it with his presence.

"Papa here?"

"He went out."

"Where?"

"He said he wouldn't be back."

His great, strong face was contorted with the pain of thought. The massive hands were helpless at his side. He said, "I was thinking I could kill Carl. Then I came to think, No, it ain't something I can do. If you like, I can go away."

He waited, fearful, searching her face. Finally, her arms went out to him.

"If he comes," she said simply, "I'll send him away. He's an animal. You're the man, no matter what I did with him. If you'll take me back?"

He put his arms about his wife and the room had the silence of peace.

The subway took him to 79th Street and Broadway. The night was warm but clouds hid the stars. It was unfamiliar territory, but a glance to the east showed the ramparts of a museum and he turned west toward the river. The street dipped toward the park and there a sedan had pulled up for a signal light.

A hard-faced man motioned him into the sedan, and made a right turn. In silence, they circled twice, before the man said, "Scarpa?"

Baldo nodded.

A package was passed. "Half passes now, half on delivery on the other side."

"I thought the whole passed."

"Half!"

"Suppose they count?"

"Half!"

Scarpa shrugged. "If no?"

"Just make it yes!"

The sedan stopped, Baldo stepped out, the sedan drove off, circled around, and came back to its original place. Baldo looked out and entered the park. A walk along an embankment ran parallel to the river. Through a rotunda of dressed stone to a boat basin on the water. In the office, he tendered a ticket given to him earlier in the day. The attendant, a boy of eighteen, checked a roster. "Okay. I'll take you out to the boat."

Baldo followed the boy out on the pier to a tender. He was helped into the rowboat where he sat in silence. The boy said, "You're sure you can manage, Pop?"

"Eh?" The question was repeated, and he turned a gaunt face of remembered fierceness. "You got your orders?"

"Sure, Pop," the boy said hastily.

"Shut the mouth!"

Oars dipped quietly into the dark water. The boy shielded his eyes, gazing off toward the blurred and dispersed neon lights across the river. "Fog."

"Never you mind."

The haze was closing the river to traffic and deep horns of ocean liners and tugs could be heard in the bay. A buoy was tolling, but his landmark, a large sign flashing on a pier, was enough for his simple navigation. That, and the bulk of a grey warship lying downriver in the center of the current. This warship, he understood, had quietly returned that day from ceremonies at a place called Newport News.

"Good night for eels," the boy remarked.

"Eels?"

"What else? Too late for the shad."

On the New York side, twin neon lights on an apartment house were navigation aides. They reached the launch dipping at anchor a small distance from the pier.

"What time do you figure to come back?" the boy asked.

Baldo's smile was wry. "Don't hold your breath."

"I'm here till morning. When you come back, flash your lights, and I'll come out for you."

"What time is it now?"

"Nine-thirty. You know how to work that launch?"

"Oh, yes! Oh, yes!"

The boy rowed back to the pier. Baldo sat for a moment, breathing heavily, and glanced about. Neither on shore nor in the river was there a sign of police. The packet of currency was a weight in his pocket—and then, momentarily closing his eyes, almost in prayer, he advanced the throttle and entered the tidal current of the river. Almost immediately, the deep tidal surge from the sea caused him to compensate as he turned down river, marking his progress by flashing signs that penetrated the fog.

Was he being followed?

He could not tell.

Then, between a huge sign flashing a demand to buy the product of a packing firm in Chicago and another cajoling a popular brand of margarine he dimly made out the dull gray hulk thrusting its snout into filthy waters. With an effort, he swung about on a diagonal and encountered the surge. He flashed a signal and a green flashed twice in response. A harsh voice called.

"*Quien va?*"

"*Amigo!*"

A flashlight painted his face and then a ladder fell down the side of the ship into the water. A man in white naval uniform descended with an air of aplomb.

"You have something for me?" said Captain Sanchez.

"Here."

Baldo handed over a package.

"Thank you, Mr. Scarpa," Sanchez said with satisfaction. "You do have a reputation, you know? And the expectation of more dealings. And this is for you." He turned about, spoke sharply in Spanish, another man in white clattered down with a large package, and the transaction had taken place.

"We are at anchor for one week," Sanchez said. "We will expect the entire matter to be closed by then. Now go with God. *Adios!*"

It was a moment of dead calm. Baldo stored the package under the seat. The engine started with a roar, it was slipped into reverse, and backed away from *Balthazar*. In moments, the far shore of New Jersey had been reached. Piers and factories loomed in the darkness as the launch picked its way past landmarks committed to memory. After two false passes, he made out a shadowy silhouette against the larger darkness of a pier.

A spotlight flashed.

"Over here! Quick, for Christ's sake!"

Baldo swung about, nodded grimly, peering into darkness. The harsh whisper came. "You got it?"

"Yes," Baldo said.

"Come here! What's holding you? You took your own sweet God damn time!"

"Too close," Baldo said. "I don't like the place."

"Why not?"

"We cross the state line, it's Federal. Let's get back to New York."

Malfino was suddenly silent. His voice changed to one of sweet reasonableness. "Look, Baldo! It's Federal anyhow, line or no line. Just let me take it."

Baldo said suspiciously, "You sure?"

"Sure!"

"Okay." Baldo smiled grimly in the darkness. "Let's stand off from the pier. I got a funny feeling, maybe you could be followed—"

"That's stupid!"

"Away from the pier," Baldo said firmly. He bore down on the wheel and started off to port.

"Baldo!" Malfino cried. "Come back! Okay, I'm coming—"

Baldo eased up on the wheel and pushed the throttle forward, glancing back occasionally at the larger, faster boat in pursuit. Malfino was standing up, outlined against a flashing sign, holding a gun—

Baldo completed a turn and headed directly for the larger boat's screw—

"Baldo, you crazy?" Malfino shouted. "What are you doing? Turn, turn! You crazy son of a bitch!"

An ocean liner's bull horn roared.

"Baldo!" Was that another voice, coming from the pier?

A stab of fire, a crack, and a spear went somewhere into the belly, a louder crash, and a vast, splintering, shattering sound that filled the sky, and then the taste of salt water and oblivion. The rattle of a whirlybird beat the waters to froth.

Baldo opened his eyes. He was weak, weak. Something held his arm. He glanced dimly and saw a tube leading to a vein. What was wrong with his breath?

"Baldo—"

He turned painfully and looked into the square, rugged face with its familiar broken nose.

"Eh? Mr. Northrup?"

"Sure."

"What happened?"

"You never left our sight."

"I squealed on Malfino?"

Northrup shook his head. "No, you killed Malfino! Not the same thing, is it?"

A smile, troubled, satisfied, played like a ghost. "No! A man does his own work. Eh?" The eyes closed, and then, "And *Balthazar*?"

"Taken care of."

"Eh, good!" Baldo painfully shifted his gaze. Helen. Jim Keleher, a big man, holding his woman, serious, calm. He came back to Northrup, sensing quiet, large men behind him. Rollins, Schreiber, the one with the Dutch name, and a captain, beyond a nurse, a man in a white coat. "Mr. Northrup?"

"Yes, Baldo?"

"I'm a four time loser."

"No, Baldo!" Northrup shook his head emphatically. "That telephone call washed you up. You don't go back."

A sad smile played, and suddenly it was not an old man. Calm summation and intelligence and purpose expressed in the gaunt features.

"—come here," said the whisper.

Northrup put his ear down.

"Up There!" The eyes looked up. "I am a four time loser. Thanks for the try." Painfully. "Send for the priest?"

"All right."

Northrup stood back and turned to Schreiber and made a suggestion in a low voice. The old man beckoned to his daughter.

"Yes, Papa!"

"Jim?"

"Here."

"Good." He rested quietly, then turned and looked into her eyes, his fingers moved feebly, and he reached out for the soft warm hair. No tears were in the grave eyes, not yet, but heartbreak below the surface.

"*Bambina!*" he whispered. "*Bambina mia!* Nothing to cry. A man is going away."

"Yes, Papa," she said. "A man."

He turned to the wall and died.

Northrup heard the click, then the familiar voice come on. "Harry, darling?" Warm, sleepy, glad.

"Donna?"

"You stood me up."

"Couldn't be helped. Could we have breakfast?"

"It's only six."

"I know, but I just saw a man die. I want to look at something beautiful, and talk. That's all."

A pause.

"Of course," she said quietly. "I'll have the coffee ready."

Northrup hung up and walked out of the hospital, passed a woman swabbing the marble floors, and into the sunlight. There would be a fresh feel in the air, he decided. He dismissed his car and set out on the long walk through deserted streets.

THE END

www.ingramcontent.com/pod-product-compliance
Lightning Source LLC
Chambersburg PA
CBHW031129210626
46816CB00015B/1249